Little Klein

Little Klein

ANNE YLVISAKER

CANDLEWICK PRESS
CAMBRIDGE, MASSACHUSETTS

I am grateful to the McKnight Foundation and the
Loft Literary Center for their generous support and to
Caitlyn Dlouhy for her vote of confidence. Many thanks to
Frank Felice, who asked for this story and discovered LeRoy,
to Uncle Don, valued reader and St. Paul's "Little Ylvisaker,"
and to my editor Deborah Noyes Wayshak, an artist.

The Inkslinger years nourished me, week by week, word by
word bucket. Olives to Lauren Stringer, Jill McElmurry,
Deb Kruse-Field, and Annie Mingo.

Special thanks to Maria for her patience and optimism,
to Darren and Carey for expanding my life, and to my posse
and my family for their care and encouragement.

First edition 2007

Library of Congress Cataloging-in-Publication Data is available.

Library of Congress Catalog Card Number pending

ISBN 978-0-7636-3359-2

2 4 6 8 10 9 7 5 3 1

Printed in the United States of America

This book was typeset in Garamond Three.

Candlewick Press
2067 Massachusetts Avenue
Cambridge, Massachusetts 02140

visit us at www.candlewick.com

For Dan Baldwin,
my heart's thesaurus

Little Klein

Little Klein was born Harold Sylvester George Klein, but his brothers had already established themselves as a group, a clump, a gang of Kleins, and being too late to be one of the older group, Harold Sylvester George Klein's given name hadn't been uttered since his baptism. Maybe the label was a jinx, a prophecy: while Matthew, Mark, and Luke were the tallest in each of their classes and always at the low end of a seesaw pair, Little Klein was barely heavy enough to make the gate swing open when he stood on its rungs.

A leaf, their mother said. *The boy is frail as a leaf; I won't get too attached to him because the next wind could blow him clear to the next county, where another mother may decide to keep him as a doll for her girls to play with.*

When Little Klein got colds, as he often did, his mother warmed the teakettle day and night, muttering as she made cup after cup of tea, *This will be his end. I'm sure of it this time. Just take him, Lord, before he gets too far stuck to my heart.*

To keep their mother from worrying all day about their little brother, the Big Kleins took Little Klein with them everywhere except school and the river. Before he could walk, they passed him from shoulder to shoulder. From this perch, Little Klein saw his first crime: shoplifting cigarettes and chewing gum from Tim and Tom's Market.

"Duck," commanded Matthew as they slipped out the door.

On a knee his second crime: taking a joyride in Officer Linden's squad car, Buddy the police dog licking his face in the backseat.

"Don't let him bite you," worried Mark.

And from under an arm his third crime: breaking into Widow Flom's house on a rainy day while she was away at her brother's.

"Slick as snot," crowed Luke as he teased open the flimsy lock. The boys spent the afternoon feasting on her state fair pie entry and last year's award-winning jam along with cheeses, root beer, and a shot of whiskey from the nearly empty bottle. This was passed over the youngest's head. Their only slip in that crime was leaving behind a diaper from the nearly four-year-old Little, which narrowed Officer Linden's search to the three hoodlums with a tot.

Though Widow Flom did not press charges (in fact, she was thrilled with what she took as a compliment to her cooking—you didn't see hungry boys breaking into Nora Nettle's house, now, did you?—as well as an omen for a good showing at the fair), Mother Klein was furious. The big boys might be spitting replicas of their father, but Little Klein still had a chance of being respectable. To expose her baby to lock picking and who knows what all, well, there wasn't enough tea in a townful of cupboards to cure that sickness.

She took Little Klein, sent the others out for Ovaltine, and locked the door. She rocked her leaf back and forth, back and forth, clutching him to her as she railed at God.

"There," she said. "You've gone and done it now. Now I full-up love this runt and you are not taking him away from me. You touch this boy and I declare . . . I'll never . . . I'll never speak to you again. Nope."

Rock, rock, rock.

"No more 'Shall We Gather at the River' for you, no more 'Praise God, from Whom All Blessings Flow.' Nope. You steal this boy from me now, and I'll take this glorious soprano you gave me and I'll lend it to Satan's show tunes.

"Got that?"

Rock, rock, rock.

"I said, got that, God?

"Humph."

Then Little Klein burped, which Mother Klein took as a sign that God had indeed relented. God had spoken through Little Klein.

After the sun went down and he begged for his brothers, Mother Klein unlocked the door and let the Bigs back in without a word.

"Sorry, Ma," said Matthew. "Won't happen again."

"I'm sorry, Mother," said Mark. "I didn't mean to. I mean I shouldn't have. I mean—"

"Sorry, Ma," interrupted Luke. "You aren't going to ground me, are you?"

"Humph," she replied, but when she tucked her smallest into the little bed next to hers and a frog jumped out from under her pillow, she laughed out loud.

"You urchins!" she called up the steps, and the next morning there was a hot breakfast on the table when they woke.

Whistlin'

Little Klein's whistling started back then, too. It was Sunday dinner, and as usual, no one could hear his thread-thin voice over his barrel-throated brothers.

"Pass the pickles," he said without result. He stretched his four-year-old arm but could reach no farther than his milk glass, and Little Klein was hungry for a Sunday pickle.

"Pass the darn pickles," he said, but even then no one heard him. Mark, the middle Big, lumped a clump of potatoes on Little Klein's plate as the bowl was passed. Little eyed the pickles in the center of the table and licked his lips. He exhaled frustration, and to his surprise a large noise whooshed out. Mother Klein put down her fork and looked around.

"Not me!" said Luke, the one usually blamed for such things.

"There is no whistling at the table," Mother Klein reminded them sternly.

Little Klein wriggled on his stack of books and licked his lips again. He inhaled. He exhaled, and this time he blew out a three-note tune.

Now everyone turned.

"Little Klein?" they gasped.

"Pass the darn pickles," he said.

Matthew and Luke bellowed, they howled, while Mother Klein stared in stunned silence and Mark simply reached for the pickles.

"Oh no you don't," said Mother Klein, swatting his hand away.

"We say 'pass.' We say 'pickles.' We do *not*, do you understand, *not* say"—Mother Klein lowered her voice to a whisper—"'*darn.*' Now. Try again. 'Pass the pickles.'"

"Pass the . . . pickles."

This sent Matthew and Luke into another fit. Mark looked solemnly at Mother, who said again, "*Please* pass the pickles."

"I'm not hungry. Can we get a god? I mean a dog? Like Buddy?"

"Most certainly not. You are much too delicate to tolerate barking and licking and fur, to say nothing of your father, who says no."

"Aw, Ma!" groaned Luke, who as the youngest Big was also the only one who got away with whining. "Dad's always got stuff to sell. He won't be home again till who knows when. What about us?"

"I may be excused," said Little Klein. He slid off his chair and stood his back up against the basement door, as was his daily habit.

"Matthew, measure him again," sighed Mother Klein. The oldest, biggest, curliest-haired Big got a pencil and a paint stick from a kitchen drawer. He held the flat stick over Little Klein's head and drew a line. Little Klein stepped out and looked. Today's line simply darkened the lines from all the yesterdays Little Klein could remember. The Matthew, Mark, and Luke lines crawled up toward the top of the door. His four-year-old line was barely higher than Matthew's two-year-old marking.

Little Klein went to sit on the front step, the farthest he could roam without supervision. He tried his pucker again. A fine, high stream spilled forth. He trilled idly, making up tunes and whistling loud as he could. He closed his eyes, breathed deep, and attempted the longest note his lungs could manage. Just when his tiny chest threatened imminent collapse, a staccato racket coming his way broke Little Klein's concentration. He opened his eyes to see four dogs coming from the east and five from the west, all barking, running . . . all going . . . wait, *coming,* right toward his yard, his step, him.

Little Klein scrambled backward, jumped for the screen door handle, missed, jumped again, and fell into the house just as the dogs crashed into the screen, yapping, barking, pleading for the whistling boy. He climbed up to look at the dogs from the safety of the other side of the door, but Mother Klein scooped Little Klein away, leaving the dogs to wrestle with one another.

While after that his body seemed to grow at the rate of a blade of grass in the shade, Little Klein's whistle flourished. Kids didn't pick on him at school because they knew that one terrible note would bring the teacher or, worse, a Big Klein running. In second grade, he was awarded the school talent trophy for his whistled medley of hymns in ragtime rhythm. And when he was nine, Little Klein's whistle roused an unsuspecting hound.

LeRoy

LeRoy lived for smelling: socks, crotches, squirrel paths, dead fish. In his dreams his nose led
him from one adventure to another. It was with
this glorious snout that LeRoy chose his family.

LeRoy had been a wanderer, a dog who
spent his nights outside the corner bar with the
other wanderers, surviving on the generosity of
the grill cook at closing time. He liked his routine, tracing the changing town smells, alley by
alley, tree by tree. Early mornings were for the
town, padding past houses as lights turned on;

midday in the cool shade by the river; afternoons smelling his way back. People he hadn't smelled much, only the storekeepers who left him scraps and the drunks leaving the bar at closing.

Then one day LeRoy's nap by the river was interrupted by an intoxicatingly sweet sound. He lifted his head abruptly, and a spindly boy tripped and landed smack on him. LeRoy rose up, the boy fell off, and the dog stuck his nose in a nest of long hair. This boy smelled of leaves and grass and rabbit and river and eggs and feet. He was a feast, but he moved fast. Soon three enormous versions of the small one grabbed LeRoy's scented boy and took him away, leaving behind a splendid bouquet of all of LeRoy's favorite smells. He yapped, he howled, he chased his tail. Then LeRoy put his nose to the ground and followed this pack.

"Get!" the biggest one yelled when he saw him catching up. "Get on, you!" LeRoy barked his most furious bark, hoping to impress. The littler boy whistled before being shushed.

LeRoy bared his teeth to show what a fine specimen he was, but the big boys ignored him. Their backs did not insult LeRoy.

"Put me down," hollered his boy.

LeRoy lagged behind while following the pungent trail out of the woods, across the bank parking lot, past Liberty Corner Restaurant (stopping not for the fine aroma of cooking cow meat), under the railroad bridge (without a glance at the yapping ball of fur in Nels Nelson's yard). He followed the pack until they walked through the back door of a house and closed it on his nose.

His long-haired boy tried to come back out to him.

"Get away from the door!" said their leader, picking up the little one like he was the weightless runt of the litter.

"I wanna keep him," said his boy, but the big one kept talking.

"Mark and Luke, get rid of the dog before Ma gets home."

"Why us?" whined one.

"I gotta work on my bike," muttered the other.

"I wanna keep him," his boy continued to plead.

"No dogs. Dad's rule and he'll be back in three weeks. Now just do it."

When the door opened and the little one popped out, LeRoy had hope, but before he could get a sniff or a lick, his boy was snatched away by the leader again.

"Beat it!" he yelled, and LeRoy scampered into the alley. He hid between garages until the streetlights came on and the house lights went out, then he crept back up to the house.

All night LeRoy lay by their step, hoping for another whiff, ear cocked for another call. His stomach rumbled, he barked, but not even the *Shad up and scram, you!* shouted out a window or the ensuing silence moved him from his spot.

After the moon rose and trash-can-scavenging raccoons woke LeRoy, he toured the fenceless yard behind the house. Weeds, rabbit, worms, raccoon, squirrel . . . but no dog. Faint whiffs, of course, faint but passing. This yard was home to no dog. LeRoy stretched. He pranced a few circles after his tail. He took a winding sniff around and around and around the house, and he knew: this was the end of wandering.

Not since his puppy days had LeRoy felt the urge to add a family to his life. But once the notion hit him, LeRoy accepted it without question. LeRoy lifted his leg on the apple tree. He went back to the dirt next to the step, where the smells of frog and ripe shoe mingled like a lullaby, and LeRoy slept.

Finders

Little Klein was the first to find LeRoy in the morning.

"My dog!" he yelled, running out the back door only to be toppled once again.

LeRoy launched into a chorus of howls and barks so long and loud that Priscilla Warren, newlywed, stepped one slippered foot onto her next-door stoop and said in her most married voice, "Well, I never!" hoping to end this uncivilized ruckus.

"Get, dog! Get on, you!" cried Mother Klein, dashing after her boy and dislodging him from the slobbering pooch. "Where in tarnation did you come from?" Then turning to Little Klein, she said, "I suppose you've been whistling again. Now, back inside. Good morning, Priscilla. New robe?" She turned toward the house. "Matthew, Mark, Luke! Up and out!"

Little Klein hesitated, and LeRoy danced around Mother Klein, knocking his boy to the ground.

"Lord have mercy!" Mother Klein cried as she separated the two again. "Boys!" she called. "Are you okay, baby?" she said, kneeling down to inspect her paw-printed son.

"Golly!" said Little Klein, diving back into LeRoy's matted coat. "I'm nine."

"You're fragile," Mother Klein answered, collaring LeRoy with her arms, pulling him away from Little Klein.

"I'm *small,* not *fragile,*" he said.

Matthew stuck his head out the upstairs window.

"We didn't bring him home, Ma. Never saw that dog before."

"Can I keep him? Can I keep him, huh? Huh, Ma? Can I keep him?" begged Little Klein.

"Certainly not. He'll break you clean in two."

LeRoy kept up his howling and barking until Mother Klein held up one hand and said, "Stop!"

Then LeRoy lay down with his head on his paws and whimpered.

"Look, Ma, he's as skinny as me," said Little Klein. "We have to feed him at least."

Mother Klein harrumphed. She called Mark to bring out a bowl of yesterday's stew. Mark set it on the bottom step before the whining dog, then walked a wide nervous circle around him. LeRoy offered the bowl three sharp barks before burying his snout and slurping it clean.

"Look at him eat," said Little Klein. "I've always wanted a dog my whole life. A dog that hungry has to be homeless."

"He's a wild dog, not a pet. Now he's fed. He's got to go back where he came from."

"No!" wailed Little Klein, planting himself on the ground next to the dog.

She waved her arms and said, "Shoo! Shoo, dog! Get on, now! Get!" But LeRoy scooted over and sniffed her feet, dribbling some undigested stew onto her shoes.

"Lord have mercy. I've got more to do with my day . . . Boys!" she yelled again.

Matthew and Luke stumbled bleary eyed into the yard, Luke mumbling, "I didn't do it," as he flopped onto the bottom step.

Matthew whapped the back of Luke's head.

"Get up," he said as he grabbed his mitt and threw a ball high in the air, watching the sky until he caught it, then threw it again.

"Mark did it," Luke tried.

"What?" Mark spun around to defend his name.

"Cut it out, Luke," said Matthew, giving him another whap, this time with his glove.

"I want to keep the dog," demanded Little Klein, but no one heard him over the ensuing Big Klein wrestling and blame calling.

When Mother Klein did not come to intervene, Mark ducked his head out of the tangle and said, "Um . . . uh . . . maybe we aren't in trouble?"

Mother now tried unsuccessfully to escort the dog from the block, Little Klein trailing behind.

LeRoy broke free and bounded back to Little Klein, then to the yard, yelping all the way.

"Do you think we'd like having a dog?" Mark asked as LeRoy and Little Klein approached, looking from Matthew to Luke.

"I've *always* wanted a dog," said Luke, grabbing a stick and throwing it across the yard for LeRoy to fetch.

"Sure we'd like a dog," said Matthew. "But we *can't* have one. Little's too fragile, for one thing." He retrieved the stick from LeRoy and threw it farther than Luke had.

"Don't blame me," said the breathless Little Klein. "Dad's allergic, when he's here. Plus he doesn't like dog smell. Come on, boy, get the stick! Just pick it up with your mouth and bring it back! Come on, boy!"

"What if he was *our* dog, the threes of us?" Mark suggested.

"There is that," pondered Luke, in rare agreement with Mark. "We could take care of it. It could be our dog, then she wouldn't worry about it hurting Little Klein." They looked to their oldest brother for the final say.

"Hey!" Little Klein tried to interrupt, but no one was listening.

"Or maybe Mark's afraid of dogs . . ."

Mark lunged at Matthew, but Luke shouted over them. "If he slept outside he couldn't bother Dad's allergies or smell up the house."

"I found him. He's *my* dog," insisted Little Klein. He tossed the stick again, but the Big Kleins were already on their way to Mother.

"Need some help, Ma?" Matthew asked.

"Mercy!" Mother Klein panted, wiping her forehead with the back of her hand. "You'll have to take it out to the woods or something."

"Uh-huh," said Luke. "But look how dirty it is. Shouldn't we at least clean it up first?"

"It's a he!" protested Little Klein, running up behind them. "Clean *him* up!"

"And," continued Matthew, "what if we keep him clean? And feed him? If he is our dog, the threes of us Bigs? We'd take care of him, make sure he stays away from Little. Keep an eye on him. Maybe he could even be some protection for Little, if we train him, like a watchdog."

"But he's *my* dog. . . ." Little Klein cried again, but Mother Klein had started resolutely singing "Onward, Christian Soldiers," which meant there was no use pleading anymore. She grabbed Little Klein's hand and huffed inside, the screen door slapping shut behind them.

LeRoy started barking all over again, bounding in circles around the boys.

"Wash the dog," she called from the kitchen window at last. "Then we'll see."

"But . . ." Little Klein headed for the door.

"There are times," Mother Klein said as she put a sheet of drawing paper in front of him, "when your brothers have things, do things, that you don't have and do. And you'll do and have things they won't. The dog is one of those things. But I'm not saying we're keeping him. In fact we can't keep him. Here," she continued from the living room, where she fiddled with the radio, "let's see if we can find a ball game. Or maybe *Captain Midnight* is on. What do you suppose that old Ivan Shark is up to this time?"

"What good's the radio when there's a live dog outside?" Little Klein moaned.

Little Klein slumped over the table. He *felt* as big as his brothers. When would his body catch up? When would he have that growth spurt his father had promised? He grabbed a pencil and drew himself as tall as the page, with a dog at his side. Around them were soaring stalks of corn, the farm Little Klein dreamed of operating. He drew in miniature farmhands, the Bigs, each smaller than the tractor far off in the field. Stanley Klein, his soon-to-visit father, was there, too, the same size as the Bigs. They were all looking up at Little Klein and his dog, smiling.

Little Klein jumped when the screen door announced Mother Klein's departure. He flipped his paper over and ran outside.

"That dog looks like your homely uncle LeRoy, may he rest in peace," Mother Klein was saying as the Bigs wrestled LeRoy into position for a rinse. "Whether or not he stays, his name is LeRoy." LeRoy woofed his approval.

"Ma!" the boys groaned. Just then the hose took an unplanned twirl, its pressure shooting water over all the Kleins, around and around until Little Klein dived onto it, taming the beast. Mother Klein turned off the hose and called, "Step away from the mud! Step back before you're all dirtier than when you started. Come inside and dry off." She turned and went inside and the Bigs sloshed after her, but Little Klein lagged back. He stood facing the wet mass of fur.

"You're a different brown now," he said.

"Woof," replied LeRoy. Then that soggy lump quaked. It shivered and twitched. The dog lowered his head and shimmied his middle, shook his rump, and let his tail swing free, releasing streams of gleaming droplets into the bright air.

Little Klein stepped toward LeRoy, his bare toes sinking into the mud. This time LeRoy didn't jump or jostle. He allowed boy fingers to comb his coat and tickle his ears. He sniffed all over his boy, lingering over the aromas caught up in the fine net of hair. Yes, this was *his* boy all right. LeRoy turned and sauntered away with the satisfaction of knowing his boy would be there when he returned.

Little Klein ran after him, but LeRoy picked up speed, turned the corner, and was gone. Little Klein dashed into the house to round up his brothers.

"For the love of Pete," Mother said. "Matthew! Mark! Luke! Get back here." But the big boys were gone, too.

Little Klein started to follow, but Mother held him back.

"Leave it to your brothers," she said. "Besides, I'm not saying we're going to keep him. In fact we can't keep him. We'll just see."

Mother set to hanging sheets on the line and singing. Little Klein climbed up the tree to watch his brothers until they were out of sight. When Mother answered Mrs. Warren's toodle-oo to help turn on her new oven, Little Klein slipped out of the yard and started running as fast as his short legs would take him after his brothers, after LeRoy.

The Bigs, not ones to run unless necessary, had slowed to a walk as soon as they were out of Mother Klein's sight, so it wasn't long before he had their curly heads in his view.

"Guys!" he shouted. "Guys!" But Little Klein's voice, a trumpet in his own head, was still a mere reed to the rest of the world's ears. So Little Klein stopped running. He filled up his chest and he whistled.

Three Bigs stopped mid-step, turned, and bellowed, "Little Klein!"

"Hey!" said Little, running up to his brothers.

"Does Ma know you're here?" asked Matthew.

"Well . . ."

"Oooh," said Luke, "you're in trouble!"

"Which means *we're* in trouble," Mark added.

Matthew picked up Little Klein and handed him to Luke. "First the dog and now him. You take him back home. We'll go find the dog."

"Hey!" cried Little Klein. "Put me down!"

"Aw, why me?" said Luke, but before he could protest further, Matthew and Mark were around the bend and out of sight. Luke threw Little Klein over his shoulder, cussing with every step toward home.

Blood trickled to Little Klein's head, which bounced upside down against Luke's back, his feet kicking desperately on the other side. "Put me down!" he yelled. "Let me come along! Put me down!"

Luke slowed a bit, but still Little Klein rode captive.

"I'm nine! Let me walk!" He pummeled Luke's back with his fists. Still Luke walked on, ignorant of the high thin voice behind him. For a while Little Klein rode quietly. Then his captor unwittingly showed him the key to his release. Luke reached back with one hand and hitched up his pants. Underwear, big Big Klein underwear, only an arm's length away. Little Klein stretched out his left arm. Jiminy! He was swinging just out of reach. Little Klein wriggled himself a little farther over Luke's shoulder and stretched again. This time he could touch the waistband but could not get enough grip to yank upward in one swift motion.

Little Klein scooted himself again. His head, now purple with pumping blood, was part of the seventy-five percent of his body hovering over Luke's back. He reached, he grabbed, he had a fistful of waistband, then "Ahhh, ahhh, achoo" sneezed hay-feverish Luke, and Little Klein's feet sailed straight over his brother's head, behind his head, below his head. Then, still holding the fistful of waistband, Little Klein was on the ground beneath a howling, cussing, red-faced Big Klein.

After much detangling, some cursory checking of Little Klein's bones, and private adjusting of Luke's undergarments, it was decided:

"You're walking the rest of the way by yourself. I'm going back to the guys, and don't even think about following me."

Luke took off at a long-legged pace, leaving his brother in a wake of dust.

"Better be quick about it, too," he called over his shoulder. "Mean Emma Brown lives around here. She'd sooner squash you than look at you."

Little Klein looked around quickly. Mean Emma Brown was supposed to be in Luke's class at school, but word was she'd been kicked out for hitting the teacher or stealing the principal's Hudson or beating up a senior. What he knew for sure was that she wasn't a town kid and her parents were dead, or she'd thrown them off a boat, or because she was ugly they'd left her with her grandpa, who didn't speak English. Little listened for heavy footsteps or yelling, but only the wind through the cottonwoods called him.

He picked his smarting self off the ground and felt a large lump grow in his throat. This was not what having a dog was supposed to be like. His dog was supposed to be his best friend, fetch things for him, sleep in his bed every night. He'd imagined himself roaming the bluffs by himself, Harold the Brave, a large and fierce canine by his side. He'd escaped the yard, caught up with the boys, and was going to rescue the dog. Yet his arms still hung like thin ropes and all his hand-me-down pants were cut off and hemmed. He still needed the bathroom light left on at night. What if all those teeth and that barking were just one more way to prove he was a baby? What if the Bigs only played with Little Klein because Ma made them? Probably a dog would be way more fun to take around than a little brother. Maybe he wasn't a real Klein at all. Little Klein took his shriveling pride and scurried himself back toward home.

He didn't have to run far. A ribbon of dust announced Mother Klein furiously pedaling her bicycle in the direction of the river, head down, hands tight on the handlebars, so focused on the road ahead that she nearly passed Little Klein waving at her from the side of the road.

Mother Klein reversed her right foot hard, jumping off her bicycle before it had fully ground to a halt.

"Mercy me," she said. "What on earth are you doing way out here?"

"I . . ." Little Klein started, pushing himself away.

"One minute you're there; the next you've blown away."

Mother Klein, with Little Klein drooping over the front handlebars, turned and pedaled home in determined silence. Priscilla Warren was waiting by the garage when they returned.

"You found him!" she cried.

"Yes," Mother Klein answered curtly as she pushed her bike into the garage.

"Wherever was he? I was telling—"

"Have you checked your meatloaf?" Mother Klein inquired of her nosy neighbor as she led Little Klein to the house.

"I . . . well, let's see . . ."

Keepers

An introvert by nature, LeRoy needed some alone time after the excitement of his first eventful morning with his family. He loped along the alleys that led out of Lena. He inhaled the world's aroma. Trash cans, cat pee, oil from leaky engines. This gave way to dusty brush and sweet wildflowers and the dark damp smell of molding leaves and rotting logs. He slowed down as he smelled the water and his own familiar scent that marked the site of his midday rests.

LeRoy rolled in the dirt and grass. He lifted his leg on a tree, then scratched his back against its bark. Once he got over the humiliation of

having his scent washed out of him in the backyard and smelled like himself again, LeRoy lay
down, closed his eyes, and slept. His dreams
tumbled with yelling boys, singing mothers,
and bowls and bowls of stew.

When he woke, LeRoy wandered the riverbank, enjoying his solitude and at the same time
anticipating returning to his boys. Today he
wandered farther than usual. He ran for a while
with another dog. They wrestled and played until the other dog got too personal and LeRoy
nipped him, ending their camaraderie. As he returned to his napping place, LeRoy saw the
Bigs sitting on a branch overhanging the river.

"This was the spot we found him. I was sure
he'd be here," said Matthew.

"No," said Luke. "Little didn't run this far. I
think he tripped over the dog back there."

"Well . . . we tried," Mark said. "We almost
had a dog. It's a stray. . . . It doesn't want to be
found. Nothing more we can do." He stood up.

"LeRoy," sniffed Luke. "Why'd she hafta pick
a name like that? It's not even from the Bible."

"Neither is Harold," added Mark.

"LeRoy," Luke scoffed.

"LeRoy," they all muttered together as they walked the balance beam of the branch toward shore.

His boys! They were calling him! LeRoy barked wildly. The boys yelled and tottered and one after another they fell off the branch and into the water. They came up howling and wet and draped themselves back over the branch like soggy laundry while LeRoy yapped and shook all over in anticipation of their next antic.

"Told you he'd be here," Matthew cried.

LeRoy yapped some more. He pranced onto the branch, promptly stepping on Mark's hands, launching him back into the drink.

"Hey!"

Then LeRoy skittered toward Luke, who dropped into the water before LeRoy could reach him. This left LeRoy sliding on the wet bark, skidding snout first into Matthew's curly head, and in they went, fur and shirt, anchors aweigh, straight to the sandy bottom, then bobbed back up to the shallow surface.

Most dogs, dropped into a lake, a pond, a river, start paddling with all four legs, running underwater. Either LeRoy was born without this instinct or it had been scared out of him in puppyhood. LeRoy bobbed and LeRoy sank.

Bob, yelp, sink. Bob, yelp, sink.

Finally Luke waded out and pulled LeRoy to shore, where he coughed out water and minnows and a leaf.

"Darn," said Matthew as the trio huddled over the quivering animal. "We finally get us a dog and this scaredy puss is it? Skinny, too." He picked up LeRoy like an overgrown baby and started walking.

"We can fatten him up," said Luke.

"What about Dad?" worried Mark.

"Hafta cure him of the willies," said Matthew. "I'm not walking around with no sissy dog."

"Woof!" LeRoy barked from the bottom of his belly, so loud that Matthew dropped him.

"Now, that's what I'm talking about, boy."

Doghouse

Ninety-one years earlier in a German forest, a sturdy oak was felled. Its trunk was sliced into boards. The boards were cut into lengths, then hammered into large boxes, which would transport the possessions of families sailing to new lives across the ocean. One of those boxes, called a trunk like its mother, was painted red on the inside and adorned on the outside with fancy scrolled figures: KLEIN 1858. It was with the boards of this trunk that the Big Kleins constructed a home for the dog that appeared to be destined to spend his nights outside.

"Why can't LeRoy sleep inside?" pleaded Little Klein. "I'd sleep better with LeRoy by my bed. He'd guard me from nightmares. We could build a tree house with those boards instead. I could see things from up there. I'd be out of your way."

"Dogs belong outside," Mother Klein answered for the fourth time that day. "He's happier outside, believe me. And you are just fine in your bed. Your father will be home in exactly two and a half weeks and he can't tolerate dogs at all, much less inside dogs. I can't believe we're keeping him this long as it is. Besides, who would call the moon if he weren't out here howling? Now, get out of the way of your brothers."

"I'd rather have a tree house." Little Klein scratched LeRoy's ears before clambering up the tree with the hammer he'd swiped from their pile. He added it to a stash he was building in a bag hung in the dense limbs. He climbed back down to LeRoy, waiting patiently at the bottom of the tree. "Let's see if we can help," he said.

"Hey," cried Matthew as they approached, "keep the dog away. He's going to mess everything up!"

"Sweetheart," Mother Klein cooed to Little Klein, "too many cooks in the kitchen and all that. Why don't you . . ."

But he and LeRoy didn't wait to hear her suggestion. They took a walk around the block, stopping for every new neighborhood smell, and when they got back, not much progress had been made.

"You're going to have to work faster than that if you want to give the dog a roof before winter," prodded Mother Klein.

"But it's only June," said Luke.

"What's Dad going to say?" fretted Mark.

"Numbskulls!" Matthew taunted. "Come on. Is anyone going to help me?"

"I'll help," said Little Klein.

"Not you," said Matthew. "You're not strong enough."

"Am so," Little Klein insisted. "Right, LeRoy?"

The Klein Boys were not used to physical labor or teamwork. "Nitwit!" was the curse of the day, and Mother Klein was fairly certain she'd have to eventually go out and just build that house herself. Other people's boys seemed to be capable—problem solvers, even. But her boys were soft from years of pampering.

Mark at least had a mind for assembly and repair—fixing neighborhood bicycles, radios, wagons, or most anything else that had come apart. But these skills gave him ideas for putting the doghouse together. He sat on the back step and sketched a plan while Matthew directed Luke to hold boards as he hammered.

"You're doing it wrong," Mark called from the top step.

"Clamp it!" Matthew and Luke retorted at once. Mark shrugged and kept working. Little Klein and LeRoy watched from the bottom step.

"Are you putting the red side in or out?"

"In," said Matthew at the same time Luke said, "Out." They glared at each other and continued working in silence.

"Okay, we're ready to nail the side boards together," Matthew said at last. "Mark, help us out here."

"You're doing it wrong," Mark said again.

"Hold on!" Luke interrupted before Mark could stir up further debate. "We aren't going to put the red part on the inside of the house, are we? Turn the side around."

"He's going to look like a sissy dog with the painted side facing out," Matthew argued.

"Luke's right," said Mark. "Red would look better on the outside. Turn it around."

Matthew's face flushed. His younger brothers were not supposed to disagree with him. He stood up. He tried again. "Inside."

"Outside."

"Inside," Little Klein called.

"Clamp it!" all three Bigs shouted up at him, and then the shoving began. Shoving led to tripping, which led to a hearty wrestle with Little Klein cheering on whoever was on top at the moment and LeRoy barking furiously.

"Nail!" screamed Luke. He held up his arm,

a nail protruding from his meaty biceps. LeRoy bounded to the injured boy, only to be swatted away.

"I win!" shouted Mark, who happened to be on top, injury being the automatic end to any match.

"Oh no," said Matthew, "I had you in a headlock. Little Klein, you call it."

"Well," said Little Klein, enjoying his moment of attention, "it depends . . ."

Luke yanked the nail from his arm and held his shirt over the bleeding part. "Ma!" he called, heading inside. "Need a bandage here."

"You see," Little Klein continued, "Mark *was* on top, but then Matthew got him in a headlock, and technically—"

"Just call it, Little Klein!" Matthew growled.

"LeRoy, you're with me, right?" Little Klein coaxed, nodding to LeRoy, who yapped back at him.

"Little Klein!" Matthew stomped toward him.

"Mark," ruled Little Klein quickly.

"Man alive!" Mark exclaimed. "I beat Matthew!" He held out his hand to Matthew. "Shake?" But Matthew had already turned back to his hammer.

Little Klein had taken one board when the trunk was disassembled. It was the one that read KLEIN 1858. Now that the house was nearly complete, he retrieved it from its hiding place behind the tree.

"You forgot something," he said. The brothers looked at the doghouse and back at Little Klein.

"Well. What should we do with this?" Little Klein displayed his find.

"We don't need it," said Matthew.

"Let's put it over the door." Mark took the board from Little Klein. "Or maybe not. It's bad enough to give the poor dog a people name like LeRoy. Dogs are not supposed to have last names."

"Aw," said Luke, returning with his arm

patched up. "I like it over the door. It'll make it look like a real house."

"We could use one more board for the ceiling, I guess," said Matthew. "Just put it on inside out. He can read to himself."

Luke grumbled but laid the board across a hole while Mark whapped a nail in either end.

The boys stood back and studied their work. They looked at one another but shared a rare moment of silence.

Mother Klein came out to inspect. "Well," she said, "it is house shaped and there is a door. . . . Is this the door?"

"Go on, LeRoy, try it out," said Little Klein, nudging LeRoy, who backed away, whimpering.

"What is everyone looking all long faced for?" said Luke at last. He stepped over to the structure. "This is a good sturdy house for LeRoy. Just because it won't win any beauty contests . . ." He leaned against the house, and with a slow creak, the whole shack leaned, too, then crackled, splintered, and crashed to the ground.

"Aw!" moaned Matthew.

"Shucks!" cried Mark and Little Klein.

"Nail!" called Luke from the wreckage, holding up his unbandaged arm.

LeRoy yapped and jumped all over Luke, trying to lick him while the Bigs helped Luke up and Mother Klein produced the iodine and bandages once again.

"Now can he sleep inside?" Little Klein implored.

"Now we start over," Mark replied.

"Start over?" groaned Matthew and Luke.

"It's wrecked," said Little Klein.

"We just need more stuff," insisted Mark, "more boards, some shingles for the roof. I made that birdhouse for Ma last year. I know more about building than you numbskulls. If you'd just listen to me—"

"Listen to you?" cried Matthew, lunging toward Mark. Luke grabbed Mark and hauled him to the ground.

"Ow!" Luke groaned. "My arms!"

"Matthew," Mother Klein broke in, ending the hubbub, "go get a dollar out of my purse. Take your brothers down to Wedge Lumber and see what you can get for it. Ask Mr. Wedge if he has any scraps out back, mismatched shingles and whatnot. Take the wagon and bring back only as much as you can haul. Any change comes back to me."

Mr. Wedge had gone to school with Stanley Klein and was disappointed to hear that Stanley wasn't around to teach his boys basic building skills. He would not take their money for a wagonload of scrap lumber and some shingles, but he did want the boys to learn how to do the job right.

"You know my boy Richard?" he asked, and they did. Rich Wedge was the only boy to have given Matthew a black eye. This earned him great respect among the Klein Boys.

Mr. Wedge opened a side door and hollered, "Richard! Come on in here!" He turned back to the Kleins as Rich ran in. "I'll give you the materials on the condition that Rich here comes along to supervise. Be apprentices this time, then we'll see about having you come back as paying customers. Deal?"

"I did sketch a building plan," Mark said quietly, but Matthew elbowed him.

"Deal," echoed the Kleins.

After a large lunch and a wrestle in the backyard, Rich and the Bigs laid out their supplies and started again. They found they liked the noise and industry of saws and hammers and the admiring remarks of Misses Lucy McCrea and Janet Wallace passing by. The Bigs were known for their pranks, and the potential for adding another dimension to their reputation was enticing.

"Yes, LeRoy, old boy," said Matthew. "You're going to be living in a palace."

Little Klein was in charge of managing the supplies and staying clear of swinging hammers. He soon grew bored. "I'd still rather have a tree house," he said, "and LeRoy can sleep in my bed."

For his part, LeRoy sauntered off for a late afternoon nap by the river. When he returned, the final nails were being hammered into his structure and this time KLEIN 1858 appeared just above the door.

How a Garden Grows

Long after moonrise LeRoy barked at the cooling air. Little Klein climbed out of bed and went outside to LeRoy. He sat on the ground in front of the dog's house and called him out. LeRoy laid his head on Little's lap.

"Look at all this yard, LeRoy. We could be growing things. Digging and planting and growing. Corn, like Farmer Filmore. You want to be a farm dog, huh? You'd like corn, wouldn't you, boy?" Little Klein scratched LeRoy's ears. "And potatoes for mashed potatoes. And pumpkins. It's not a very big yard, LeRoy, but we could do it. Couldn't we, boy? Couldn't we? I'm not too small for growing things, am I? Think about it, LeRoy. We could sell our harvest to Tim and Tom's Market. We'd be rich!"

LeRoy howled his agreement, woofed his delight with the moon, his yard, his boy.

"Go back to sleep, LeRoy, and quit barking at the stars. They are not coming down no matter how much you beg."

Little Klein went back inside and slept soundly until morning.

Everyone was sitting at the table when he padded out to the kitchen. Mother sat down, too.

"Can I plant some things in the backyard?" he asked.

"Gardens are for sissies," mumbled Luke through his cereal.

"Corn is not—" Little started but then paused when Mother Klein seemed to be considering his plan.

"Hmmm . . ." she said, getting up to turn off the teakettle, "I've been thinking about gardening myself. I'm glad you reminded me. I want a flower garden. Flowers to balance all the boyness around here. Cosmos, daisies, zinnias. Roses. It's a little late to start planting, but why not? I may need a book or two and yes, roses as well. Your father will be home in two weeks and the yard should look fine. That doghouse sticks out as it is. Today's as good as any to get started. Finish up, boys. You're going to help me."

"But . . ." started Little Klein, "I meant . . ." but Mother Klein was already out the door.

She took her teacup and wandered through the yard, pacing it off end to end, side to side. She looked at her square of land as a farmer does in the spring. She saw red and yellow. She saw neighbors stopping to admire. Mother Klein saw herself in a bonnet with a hoe and she saw herself at the state fair with blue ribbons and her name card, *Esther Klein,* paired proudly.

She could bring bouquets to neighbors who would invite her in for lemonade. The women who entered produce, baked goods, and such in the county fair talked all the time and even rode together to the city for the state fair judging. By the time the boys came out for instructions, Mother Klein had a plan.

"We need a ball of string and the croquet set. We need the paper off some sticks of gum and a pencil. Go round up those things, and then you're going to the library."

The library? Their eyes widened. They groaned.

"I don't want to hear another word. I'll do the dishes while you find everything."

"But Mother, I wanted . . ." Little Klein tried again.

"Woof," said LeRoy. "Woof."

"You can help your brothers or dry the dishes," said Mother Klein, distracted. Little Klein wandered off to the garage, LeRoy at his heels. What about his corn and potatoes and his pockets heavy with coins?

When the kitchen was clean, Mother Klein stood in front of her curious boys and plucked supplies one by one. First she wandered around the yard, taking long paces and randomly poking croquet hoops into the ground. Then she tied one end of the ball of string to a corner hoop and walked from hoop to hoop, tying one to another until the yard was a grid, a map of little states of different shapes and sizes.

"Don't ask yet," she said as she untied and retied until the map met her satisfaction. LeRoy paced the small section that surrounded his house, whimpering and afraid to cross the line.

"Oh, for Pete's sake, haven't you ever seen string before?" Mother said. "Go on down to the river for your nap, why don't you." But LeRoy couldn't get himself to step over those strings. Finally, she lifted his front legs, then his back legs, and shooed him to the alley, where LeRoy looked forlornly back at her. Where was his calm, singing mistress? Who was this scurrying woman with the sharp voice? When she didn't answer his cries, LeRoy turned and plodded off to the river, not stopping to enjoy the ripening smells of things in decay.

Back in the yard, Mother Klein chewed on the pencil as she studied her states.

"I don't know what we're going to do with that dog when your father comes home," she muttered. Then "Roses," she finally declared, and reached for a gum wrapper. ROSES, she wrote on the wrapper. She gently lifted the leg of a hoop and threaded the paper onto it. She walked to a long skinny state near the house.

"Cosmos," she said. "Zinnias." She reached for two more papers and threaded these both on one hoop. The largest state she labeled DAISIES. When mums and heliotrope had also been given statehood, she turned to the boys.

"What do you mean, 'what we're going to do with that dog'?" Mark asked.

"Your father's sensitive to barking," said Mother. "And he doesn't like dogs and that's that."

"One more," she said. "Any ideas?" The usually rambunctious boys had been stunned into near lethargy and were watching their mother from under the tree.

"Well?"

"Pickles," said Little Klein.

"Everyone in agreement?" she asked.

"Can't grow pickles," scoffed Luke.

"It all starts with cucumbers," said Mother Klein, "and cucumbers we can do." She wrote PICKLES on the last wrapper, then stuck a croquet hoop through it and into the ground.

Hush

The most disturbing thing about the library was its lack of sound. To boys used to the continuous racket of their own company, the hush of the library was as frightening as a looming pack of boys was to the librarian. Fragrant summer air swirled in when the boys stumbled through the door. It hung around them for a moment before being absorbed by the somber book air that had lived in the library for the eternity of its existence.

Miss Muriel glanced up from the card catalog where she was helping Janet Wallace find a book on bees. Mr. Olafson paused over the *Farmer's Almanac.* Reverend Clambush looked up from a stack of gardening books from which he was gathering metaphors for his sermon, and The Reverend Missus Clambush lowered the book she was using to disguise her interest in the activities of Widow Flom, who was perusing the fiction section. LeRoy's barks floated through the open window.

"Let's ask *her,*" said Little Klein in his outdoor voice, pointing a dirt-crusted finger at The Reverend Missus Clambush, whose trim hat and suit gave an official air.

"SHHHHHHhhhhhhhhhhhh," said everyone at once as Cornelia Clambush guiltily dropped her book and looked behind her to discover at whom these ruffians were pointing.

"No," said Luke in what he supposed was a whisper. "That's her over there." He pointed his own crusty claw at Muriel, who shut the card drawer on her finger. As the gang of Kleins tromped the fourteen paces to the reference checkout desk, no one went back to their reading.

Miss Muriel looked at the Reverend, trying to send him a signal to pray for her. The sight of three broad and scruffy boys was not tempered by the scrawny one at their side. While Muriel had weathered any number of unusual patron requests in her three-week tenure as a professional librarian and even a storm that blew out the west window, she had not yet faced imminent bodily harm from a pack of hoodlums.

She grabbed the dictionary, held it in front of her face, and, when the biggest asked, "Ummm?" she whimpered, "Take anything. There's no money in the building, but take anything else you want, only please don't hurt me. And please leave *Jane Eyre* as it is my favorite."

The boys shuffled from foot to foot, not sure how to respond to her request, until Widow Flom laughed. Out loud.

"Muriel," she screeched in between guffaws, "Muriel, may I introduce the Klein Boys. Boys, this is Miss Muriel, our new librarian." That was as far as she could get before she had to flop down in a chair with her handkerchief and let the fit take her over. The sound of Widow Flom's laughter was like a drug wherever she used it, and soon the entire patronage of Lena Library was giggling, hiccing, tittering, and out-and-out laughing. The Klein Boys joined in, too, imagining themselves stars in some grand joke they hadn't known they'd planned but would take the credit for nonetheless.

"Muriel," Widow Flom finally continued, "your job is to serve. Won't you ask these gentlemen what they need?"

Muriel, who had allowed herself a few self-conscious titters, lowered her dictionary and asked in as librarianish a voice as she could muster, "May I help you, Misters Klein?"

"Yes, please. Our mother sent us here to check out some books. She is planting flowers in our yard, and we need to know . . ." Mark held out his hand to Little Klein, who gave him a piece of paper and a library card. "We need to know, 'How far apart do you plant zinnia seeds?

How much sun do cosmos require? What does one feed roses and which ones grow best in northern climates?' And, um, what is a heliotrope?"

"And allergies," added Little Klein hastily. "We need a book about allergies."

The Reverend Mrs. Clambush could be silent no longer. "A garden!" she exclaimed. "Why, you can't learn gardening from a BOOK! No offense, Muriel, but BOYS! Where do you LIVE? Now, PEOPLE!" this addressed to the patrons who had not returned to their reading material, "The mother of these boys is in NEED. Put down your BOOKS and follow ME."

Cornelia Clambush thrust her book at Muriel and with a sweeping motion gathered the entire Saturday population of Lena Library into a reluctant huddle around the Klein Boys. "We are being CALLED to SERVICE this day. BOYS, lead us home."

Muriel hastily produced *Gardening Basics* but had to stay at the library to cover the desk.

"No!" the boys cried at once.

"Well!" huffed Cornelia.

"What we mean is, that's okay, Mrs. Clambush," said Matthew as politely as he could manage. "We'll take it from here."

Progress

Cornelia Clambush did not accompany them home that day, but she soon found occasion to be in the Klein neighborhood.

"Boys!" she sang in two syllables as they tossed a football in the street. "Is your mother at home? I divided my hostas and must find someone with space in their garden. You can go get them and bring them here. We'll go ask her now, shall we?"

While his brothers trudged off to the parsonage, Little Klein watched from the tree, LeRoy keeping guard underneath as Mother and

The Reverend Missus toured the garden. When they got to the PICKLES sign, Cornelia paused. "You can't grow pickles, dear."

Mother Klein bit back her instinctual reply, breathed deeply, and said simply, "It's cucumbers, of course, but my youngest wanted a garden, too, so I let him choose something."

"Oh yes, you're wise to encourage their ambitions. Why, my Barbara is the toast of Owatonna with her elegant dinner parties. Don't you know I encouraged her from the start, letting her set the table when we had guests, fill the glasses, all kinds of grown-up responsibilities. I believe my Barbara owes a great deal of her prowess in the kitchen to childhood observation and prodding. Now, Esther, you've got a fine start here, but if I could offer some suggestions . . ."

Little Klein dropped from the tree, whispered "Stay" to LeRoy, and attempted to cross to the house unnoticed. If there was one thing that put his mother in a bad mood, it was unsolicited advice.

"There's the cherub!" trilled Cornelia Clambush. "Come here and let me have a look at the little farmer."

Little Klein approached her slowly, glancing at the street, willing his brothers' return.

"I was just showing The Reverend Missus . . ." his mother was saying.

"My Land! There's no call for such formality! Call me Mrs. Clambush, dear."

Mother Klein started again. "Mrs. Clambush and I were just admiring the progress in your pickle garden."

"Thank you," said Little Klein, seizing the opportunity to use a previous lesson on making polite conversation. "Corn would be nice, too. I was really hoping to grow corn."

Mother Klein smiled too widely and gave Little Klein the *That's enough* eye. "Guess he was born to be a country boy. I was hoping you'd tell me more about your Barbara—"

"Corn?" interrupted Mrs. Clambush. "Why, Mrs. Klein, you don't need to plant an acre for the boy. One stalk here in this sunny spot will do. I'll send the Reverend over tomorrow to help him get started."

LeRoy bounded over to Little Klein. "Shhh, boy," he said as he looked from his mother to Mrs. Clambush, cautious in his hope for his own corn.

"The boy can poke a hole in the dirt by himself just fine, thanks just the same," said Mother Klein, the angry vein on her neck popping out as a warning no one but her boys could read. While Cornelia Clambush paused, deciding whether or not to be offended, Mother Klein recovered her decorum.

"Of course, you and the Reverend are welcome to stop by anytime to check in on progress. Or for any other reason. I am Lutheran, though I have slipped in attendance and sometimes go over to the Methodists. Have you heard their new preacher? Really, I am a Conversationalist, one who converses with the Higher Up. I certainly have nothing but respect for you Episcopalians." Mother Klein wiped her forehead with her sleeve.

"We're Presbyterian, dear," corrected Mrs. Clambush, "but I'm sure the corn is nondenominational."

As the grown-ups went inside for iced tea, Little Klein, with LeRoy on his heels, raced to the garage for a trowel. He dug a hole in the discussed spot before Mother Klein could change her mind. He slipped into the kitchen, grabbed three forks, and stuck them in the ground around the hole, then tied string around the forks, marking the territory. He made a label, CORN, and sat waiting for his brothers, LeRoy at his side.

The Minister

Little Klein longed to fish with his brothers but was considered a drowning risk by his mother. Days of sighing about the wait for his corn to grow, though, frayed Mother Klein's patience, so as a distraction she let the Bigs take Little Klein to the river at last.

"Keep LeRoy close," she cautioned, unaware of LeRoy's unusual swimming affliction.

The Bigs tied a hook on a string on the end of a stick and deposited Little Klein on a spot of sandy shore. They drifted off to the ledge that reached out over the river, LeRoy panting behind them. The Bigs dropped their lines with reels and real coated fishing line.

In the river just below the ledge, a deposit of stones made an underwater cove where the fish of Klein dreams lived. The boys called him The Minister because they'd first seen him on a Sunday morning and he'd slapped the water loud as the preacher'd pounded the pulpit on Easter. Ten years ago someone had pulled a 137-pound catfish from this river. The Minister could be their fame.

While the Klein Boys hadn't caught a really large fish in the river, a baited hook had not gone uneaten until they met The Minister, an over-grown catfish that'd lost his traveling spirit and lived a hermit's life in this shallow stretch of river bottom where he grew fat and lazy eating unsuspecting delicacies that floated by. The Minister had seen enough of his mates yanked out of the water by ugly mugs like those peering at him over the ledge that he proclaimed a diet anytime their shadows disturbed his watery den.

Little Klein stood in the weeds dangling his

line near the shallow shore while his brothers baited The Minister and forgot about him. They certainly did not expect him to catch anything. Distracted by a squirrel, LeRoy wandered into the woods.

Little Klein held his line steady for a bit, then jigged it, making the dead worm wriggle in what he considered an appetizing way. He imagined himself mess cook, feeding worms to an army of fish. He'd reel them in, caught on his line like ribbons on a kite string. There'd be a town fish fry to cook up his catch. "Who caught all these fish?" people would ask and he would hear his name, Harold Klein, murmured through the crowds. "That's my boy," his father would tell people. "That's my boy and his dog." Little Klein pulled his line along as he walked the shore, then repeated his dangling, jigging, and dragging. He was rewarded with a tug on his line.

"Got one!" he yelled, hanging on to his stick as he ran along the shore in the direction the fish was pulling his line.

"Set your hook!" called Matthew, sliding down from the ledge on his bottom.

"Pull your stick up!" added Mark.

Little Klein yanked his stick, and with a snap he was left with a six-inch twig while his line and the rest of his stick followed the escaped fish.

They went home with an empty net that day, but Little Klein was hooked on fishing. He relived that moment when the fish pulled at his line over and over. The stick had been weightless in his hands and then like a divining rod had jerked and pulled like a thing alive. In those few seconds a rush of excitement flew from his hands up his arms, through his body, and right out his toes, and he wanted more.

"I need a fishing pole," Little Klein announced at dinner that night.

"Can't one of you boys share?" Mother implored, looking from Matthew to Mark to Luke. They stared back at her as though she'd asked them to share their underwear. "Okay, all right. We'll see."

After dinner, Mother Klein poked around in the garage. She sorted through shovels, rakes, and old brooms. Then, mixed in with a pile of skis, she found it—a tall bamboo pole. She wrestled it free and leaned it against the house.

"There," she said to Little Klein, who was watching behind her. "Have your brothers tie some fishing line on there and you're all set."

"Man alive!" exclaimed Little Klein, picking it up and swinging it around, accidentally catching the back of Mother's dress, then whapping LeRoy.

"Oh!" he cried.

"Careful! Don't you go hurting anyone with your father coming home in eight days, no . . . seven. You'd better just leave that pole by the house until your brothers can help you." She paused. "Maybe it is too big. . . ."

"No! I'll be careful! It's perfect, Ma."

The next day they set off for the river again. LeRoy and the Bigs gathered around Little Klein on the shore with instructions.

"One: Don't pussyfoot around when you get a nibble."

"Woof!"

"Two: Don't pull up too fast. Let 'im get the hook all the way in his mouth."

"Woof!"

"Three: Set the line." This with the yanking of an imaginary rod and a snap of wrists.

Wagging tail.

"And four: If you're going to be a real fisherman, you have to bait your own hook."

"Woof! Woof! Woof!"

Luke pulled a fat earthworm from the can they'd filled after dark the night before and tore it in half. "No use givin' 'em a whole juicy guy like this if they're not going to get a chance to digest it anyhow. All you need is a tantalizing sample. Want the other half, LeRoy?"

With a clump of oatmeal suddenly squirming in his stomach, Little Klein held his breath and threaded his hook.

"There you go! Toss it out."

LeRoy and the Bigs sat down on the bank to

watch Little Klein and offer tips. The bamboo pole was twice Little Klein's height and the line twice again as long, so a new method of casting was devised. Little Klein laid the line out along the edge of the water and the pole after it. He walked back to the hook end of the line and tossed it in the water then ran back to the pole end, lifting it from the middle and rotating it out over the water.

When he grew tired of standing and jigging the worm, he sat cross-legged on the sand, his eyes not leaving the tip of his pole. The suspense of the first cast over, the Bigs argued over what new bait might tempt The Minister today, the merits of a cube of cheese being weighed against a wooden red spinner. LeRoy sauntered into the trees for a sniff around. The weight of the long pole having tired Little Klein's jigging arm, he let the line float off downstream and his attention drift.

The Minister was returning to his rocky den after his morning laps around the area and was surprised to see a snack resting right there on his floor. He rolled his eyes up to the ledge. No large-eared creatures peering over. A snack, free and clear, and he hadn't had a worm in oh, so long. Ordinarily he would have been more cautious, but an annoyingly sociable carp had been dropping in lately and The Minister was not about to share, so with a greedy gulp he swallowed that half worm whole and settled in for a nap.

At that same moment Little Klein decided to try his luck upriver a ways. He lifted his pole and turned to take it with him. Shoot. His hook must have snagged. He yanked. The Minister woke with a sharp pain in his belly and that annoying carp watching him with her watery lovesick eyes. He tried to burp the pain out and was nearly successful, but then it lodged itself in his lip.

The Minister lurched about, trying to free himself of the pain. The carp came at him, wanting to help, and with a furious exhalation of bubbles The Minister showed her his back fin as he swam away in a panic. On the other end of the line, Little Klein felt not the pleasing tug of the fish he'd nearly caught on the stick but a yank that nearly stole the rod from his hands.

"Bite!" he screamed, gripping his dancing pole. Little Klein dug his heels in the sand and skidded down the shore, caught as much by The Minister as The Minister was caught by him. And then he was in the water, skipping along the surface but not letting go.

"Bite!" he called again when he could get his face out of the water. Ahead of him, The Minister sped toward a submerged tree root, braced himself, and snagged the line he knew was trailing him. With a rip he left the hook and part of his lip behind and was free. He swam unsteadily back to his den, snuggled himself under a rock, and, without the energy to dismiss the loitering carp, The Minister slept.

As the line went slack, Little Klein sank. Matthew, Mark, Luke, and LeRoy ran along the shore after him. The boys dived into the river and pulled Little Klein out, still clutching his rod.

"Tip number five: Let go of the rod before it pulls you in."

"Woof!"

"He got away," mourned Little Klein as he examined the dangling line. "He must have been enormous. I'll bet it was The Minister."

"Nah. The Minister never eats worms."

A Pair of Shiny
New Shoes

The Bigs used to be tree climbers, but as they'd grown tall, they'd grown heavy. The backyard pine was a testament to their girth, with its shattered lower limbs. Only Little Klein could navigate the nubs of these former branches, shinnying up to higher limbs to keep lookout whenever needed.

Today, Little Klein was watching for Stanley Klein, returning father and husband, as well as allergic and uninformed owner of a dog named LeRoy.

LeRoy howled at the base of the tree.

"Take that dog somewhere today," Mother Klein ordered the Bigs as she weeded her garden. "He can't be here when your father arrives."

"Ma!" whined Luke.

"Go on, guys," said Little from high in the branches. "I'll come find you after Dad gets here."

"Oh sure. When after? Tomorrow? I don't think so," said Mathew, Luke grunting his solidarity.

"Mercy, Lord, you gave 'em to me," pleaded Mother Klein with the sky. "You should have dealt me more patience while you were at it." She drew her small frame to its full height and turned to the Bigs. "Boys, take LeRoy and find somewhere you haven't been before. . . ."

"She means get lost," muttered Luke.

"Go," finished Mother Klein.

Little Klein watched the road from between the branches. The last time his father had been home was four months ago, and he was sure he'd grown since then. There had been a snowstorm that kept the boys home from school.

Mother was afraid the snow was too deep for Little Klein, but Father had said, "Let him go play, Esther. Just put a red hat on his head. He won't disappear." Little Klein's heart swelled for his father then. His father thought of him as one of the boys. But outside the snow *was* deep, and it was sticky, too. The way it stuck to Little Klein's pants and jacket and mittens gave Luke an idea. By the time Father Klein came out looking for him, Little Klein had been rolled into a snowman. Only his wildly flapping hands and the hole revealing his frozen face gave him away. Instead of punishing the Bigs, Father Klein had laughed. He'd hooted. He'd chipped Little Klein out of his snow wrapper, tears running down his face, and called him his little elf.

This time would be different. Now Little Klein had bigger stories to tell. He had fish tales. His corn stalk was emerging. They had a dog and he got to be the one to deliver the news. His father would let him keep LeRoy once he met him and found out what a good dog he was. He hooked his knees over a high branch and dangled upside down while he watched cars approach and pass the house. Little Klein watched until the noon whistle blew in town, until his head was heavy with the blood all draining south, until it was so heavy in fact that when he reached up to grasp a branch to pull himself up again, he slipped and fell through branches, which slowed his fall but didn't stop it until he landed facedown on a bed of pine needles and a fresh heap of LeRoy doo. He pulled at a pine needle in his ear and groaned as he rolled over.

"There's *one,*" said a voice attached to a pair of shiny new shoes.

"Dad!" coughed Little Klein as he pulled himself up then fell back.

"Ooff," he said, lying on his back, resting a hand on his stomach, and encountering the smelly LeRoy paste. "Ick!"

Stanley crouched down and peered at Little Klein's face. "You all right, Little Guy? Can you get up?" He turned toward the house. "Esther! You in there? Boy's hurt out here! Esther!"

"Dad, I'm okay," huffed Little Klein as he rolled over to his side and slowly pulled himself up to sitting.

"There," said Stanley, moving back a little. "There now. Thatta boy."

"My baby! Stanley? Is that you? He fell out of the tree? Heavens to Betsy! Is he broken?"

"Since when do you let him climb trees?"

"Don't pick him up yet. He could have injured his back or neck." Mother Klein knelt next to Little Klein while Stanley stood awkwardly by.

"I'm fine," said Little Klein, swiping a palm across his face, spitting, and struggling to his knees.

"He's fine," echoed Stanley Klein.

But Mother Klein picked him up and his face went red.

"Hi, Dad," he said as they swept past Stanley and into the house, where he was propped on the couch with blankets and pillows while Mother Klein scrubbed at his head with a wet cloth. Stanley sat in a side chair and waited for Esther's attention.

"Where are the boys?" he asked.

"Oh, they'll be back in a bit," she said, and they launched into an exchange of adult talk that left Little Klein out. Here he was on the couch like a baby, like nothing had changed, but things had changed, if only his father would see. Right this minute there were no Bigs in the house to distract his father from his youngest son. This was Little Klein's opportunity to have his father's sole attention.

"We got a dog!" he interjected at last. Silence was not the expected reaction, so he continued. "His name is LeRoy and we built him that house that's in the backyard and he—"

"You have what?" Stanley exclaimed, rising slowly, his eyes darting around the living room as if the dog would appear from behind a chair or picture frame. "You can't have a dog," he said finally as he dropped into his chair. "No dogs. Absolutely not. Get the notion out of your head, boy."

Stanley turned back to his conversation with

Mother Klein, who scrubbed Little Klein's head harder.

"Ouch!" he said. "But we *do* have a dog and his name is LeRoy and he'll be back soon and you'll meet him." This time the silence was much shorter. Stanley looked at Esther, who was giving her sternest eye to Little Klein, who said, "What?"

"You're right," said Mother Klein. "You do look fine. Go back outside now and wait for your brothers."

"But I—"

"Go."

Little Klein trudged as far as the back door, which he opened and closed, and then tiptoed back in to listen.

The Fugitive and
Widow Flom

Little Klein was not allowed to be superstitious. Mother Klein blessed his head every morning, and according to her, luck had nothing to do with his head resting safely on his pillow at night.

But today, listening in from the kitchen to his parents talking about LeRoy, he remembered about the mirror.

"Can't have a dog here," Stanley was repeating.

". . . protection . . . no harm . . ."

Last week when the Bigs were wrestling their way through the front door, they'd knocked the mirror off the entry wall. Mother Klein had simply dealt out broom, dustpan, and bandages while Little Klein counted slowly, realizing his brothers would be living out in the world on their own before they'd be free of the seven-year spell he wasn't supposed to believe the mirror held.

The next day Matthew and Luke conked heads so hard their eyes may have leaked, they threw up, and Dr. Dahlke had to be called. While the doctor pulled at their eyelids and shone a thin light in their pupils, diagnosing concussions, Little Klein studied Mark, who didn't look so big without his flanks and imagined what a thin pair they'd be alone. So sure was he that his conk-headed brothers were catching the train to Saint Peter's pearly gates that when a spider dropped from the ceiling at the moment the injured sat up to argue, Little Klein saw it as an eight-legged sign of good fortune, a reduction of the mirror's sentence. But once his relief wore off, Little Klein forgot about the mirror, superstition, and bad luck.

"He's going to the pound and that's all there is to it."

The mirror, it seemed, had not loosed its curse.

Little Klein had to find his brothers before they brought LeRoy home.

The boys had started walking in the direction of downtown and why not? On the way they could chance meeting Lucy or Janet. There was Anderson Park for running little kids off the monkey bars and winding the swings over the top bar. Once downtown, there was Mildred to tease and sodas at Nile Drug. Little Klein became so involved in imagining the adventure of finding his brothers that he did not hear the voice until it was shouting at him: "Hey, Klein boy!"

Little Klein looked up. He looked in front of him, behind him, then again the unfamiliar voice bellowed, "Over here, runt!"

Little Klein's eyes followed the voice across the street. There stood Mean Emma Brown, the tallest girl he'd ever seen, her hair in shock on all sides, men's boots on her feet, legends of her nasty temper generating an aura about her.

"Ain't Luke Klein your brother? I'm looking for him."

Little Klein didn't pause to answer. He turned and ran, zigzagging through the neighborhood, feeling her close behind him but hearing nothing.

He didn't see Widow Flom until he ran flat into her.

"Harold Klein!" she said.

"Sorry, ma'am!" He looked behind him at the vacant street, then slid around to stand on the other side of Widow Flom.

"Does your mother know you are out wandering the streets alone?"

"Well, I . . . she . . . I mean . . . my dad . . ."

"Your father? Is he home?"

"Yes, ma'am."

"Does he know you are out wandering the streets alone?"

"I . . ."

"Come with me," Widow Flom boomed.

She took Little Klein's hand and led him up the steps to her porch. "Sit down right here. Your mother must be worried sick. I know for a fact she doesn't let you roam about by your lonesome. Your father, I have no idea, but if he's home, Esther has enough on her plate without worrying about you. And speaking of plates, I'll run inside and get you a slice of pie—looks like you could use some pie—then off we go, young man. I'll ring your mother and let her know you're safe."

Little Klein could have used a piece of pie after the Emma Brown incident, but he remembered the purpose of his mission and opened his mouth to stop her. Widow Flom was in the house and picking up her hallway phone before his voice could catch up. He pushed through the door and grabbed the phone from its stand and with it the receiver from Widow Flom's ear.

"Wait!" he said in the voice he'd finally found.

Widow Flom stood in stunned silence, her empty hand still raised to her ear.

Encouraged by his rapt audience, Little Klein continued, telling Widow Flom about LeRoy's impending fate and the need to find the Big Kleins and LeRoy before they went back home.

"Well," said Widow Flom when she'd regained her composure, "if I must pay a ransom for my phone, I must."

Little Klein flinched at the sight of a telephone in his arms and nearly dropped it. He'd been so intent on getting Widow Flom's attention that he'd forgotten he was still holding it. Grasping the phone firmly to his chest, Little Klein began again, "I . . ."

"Here is what I am prepared to offer. In exchange for my telephone, I will harbor said fugitive canine until all parties have been heard and all parties have come to a mutually agreeable resolution."

"What?" said Little Klein.

"I'll keep your dog here until your parents sort things out. Now, come on. We'd better find the boys before they get home. We may already be too late."

Little Klein turned to go.

"The phone?" prompted Widow Flom.

Little Klein set the phone on its stand and followed Widow Flom out the back door and climbed into her car. He sat in the front seat, looking out cautiously for LeRoy and the boys and terrified at the possibility of seeing Emma Brown.

They drove down Walnut, up Maple, across Plum, and toured slowly down Main, and there she was, walking away from them. Little Klein slumped down in his seat, barely breathing.

"You aren't going to see them from down there, that's for certain. We'd better circle back closer to your house," suggested Widow Flom. "If we stay nearby, we'll have a better chance of intercepting them."

Little Klein waited until the car had made a couple of turns before he pulled himself back up and started watching again.

Sure enough, as the car coughed its way up the Maple hill, there was a leaping, yapping dog, bounding its way around three strapping boys. Widow Flom tooted her horn and pulled over beside the boys.

"Hold up there, boys. Meet your brother and me in my kitchen. Go on inside." She winked. "It's not locked. The dog can come in, too. Just keep his snout off the counter."

"Thanks, Mrs. Flom, but we've got to get home. Another time," said Matthew.

"This is not a social invitation, young man. I will see you in my kitchen."

Four boys arrived home for supper that night without their dog. If their parents noticed, neither one mentioned the fact. Dinner conversation centered around Stanley—stories of his sales, his travels, people he'd met, places he'd stayed, unusual sights he'd seen, places he promised to take them all someday.

That night the doghouse stood empty. When Little Klein crept downstairs to get a glass of water, he peered out at the dogless yard and scanned for signs of a tall girl in boots hiding in the bushes or near the garage. He crawled back into bed feeling every ounce of his smallness.

Mother Klein lay on her side, watching the moonlit yard, hoping that wherever LeRoy had been during the day, he would leave it and return home by morning.

Widow Flom snored on through the long hours of LeRoy's pacing and whining, through his kitchen foraging and toilet water slurping.

Stanley Klein simply slept.

Too Much Mollycoddling

Morning broke cloudy and barkless. Stanley studied his glum boys around the breakfast table. His eyes traveled from tallest Matthew to broadest Luke to muscular Mark then down to the pencil-armed Little Klein, shoveling oatmeal into his small "o" mouth as fast as his spiny hand would travel. Stanley stopped eating and frowned.

"Is he getting enough to eat?" Stanley asked of no one in particular.

Mother Klein followed Stanley's eyes to Little Klein.

"Of course. Look at him go."

"Has he been sick?

"No. What's the problem?"

"He hasn't grown at all since I saw him last."

"He's our frail one, Stanley."

Little Klein held his spoon still and looked up.

"I have so grown. You can check the grow lines on the door."

"Nine years, Esther. I think the boy is out of the woods; he's not going to die a feeble infant. What we have here is the product of too much mollycoddling." Stanley pushed away from the table and paced around it as six bowls of oatmeal grew cold. "Enough. While I'm home these next two weeks, we're going to start toughening him up." He looked at the Big Kleins, who refused to meet his eyes. "And I'm going to need everyone's help." The Bigs folded their arms across their chests without comment.

Mother Klein stood with two hands on Little Klein's shoulders.

"He'll grow when he's good and ready."

"When's LeRoy coming home?" pestered Little Klein.

"Forget about that dog for a minute and concentrate, Big Guy," his father admonished.

Big Guy. Little Klein hesitated. Toughen him up. Little Klein imagined himself running with the rough crowd, sporting a black eye, muscles bulging out of his shirtsleeves.

"What exactly would we be doing?" he inquired hesitantly. The Bigs glared at him for breaking their silent treatment in support of LeRoy.

"Now you're coming around," Stanley exclaimed, rubbing his hands together. "We'll start with strengthening. Things like pull-ups. You're going to have to eat better, too."

"He's our youngest, Stanley. Why rush things?" Mother Klein countered.

"Matthew, Mark, and Luke aren't going to be around here forever," Stanley said. "Fact, when I left Chicago, Mr. Huppert said they're looking for fresh young men in St. Paul, and I told him my Matthew was a smart one with only a year left in school."

Now it was Matthew who couldn't contain himself. "Really? What would I sell?" He remembered himself and looked back down at the table.

"Don't you bring Matthew into it," retorted Mother Klein. "You can go ahead with Little Klein's exercising and whatnot on one condition, Stanley. The dog stays."

Everyone looked at Stanley, who looked at the floor, at the sink, at the window, and at the ceiling for a very long moment.

"No dogs. That's the rule," he said, but Mother Klein only raised her eyebrows while the boys waited expectantly.

"You know I don't like dogs," he continued. "I'm allergic," he tried. Still Mother Klein stood silent. The clock ticked like hand claps, endless spaces between the beats; a shuffled foot was sandpaper; coughs echoed as in a canyon. Even Stanley was no match. There was nothing louder than Mother Klein's quiet.

"Go find your dog," he said at last, then muttered, "Maybe I'll have to get back to work sooner than I thought."

Little Klein followed his brothers to Widow Flom's house for the reunion with LeRoy. LeRoy, while glad to see his boys, was distracted. He had a new love and her name was strawberry pie. He had his snout deep in a slice of heaven when they burst through the door. But a few minutes of rough and tumble worked LeRoy back to his frisky self, and after the boys had eaten the rest of the pie, the whole outfit ambled back home.

Little Klein lagged behind a ways. He watched his legs as they took turns striding in front of him. He bent one forearm, then the other, trying to show a biceps muscle. He had his brothers to protect him. How much toughening did he need? What were they going to do to him?

Stanley was waiting for them by the laundry line in the backyard. The yard was nothing like he'd keep it if he lived here full-time. What had gotten into Esther? Used to be a fellow could count on a nice plot of green divided by a neat concrete path to his driveway and his garage. Look at this unconventional mess: his lawn broken into ribs of flowers and a muddy patch where the doghouse stood. If it weren't for space around the laundry line, he'd have no room to roam about. LeRoy broke away and ran right up to Stanley, sniffing him in an exceedingly impolite manner.

"LeRoy!" cried Little Klein, and pulled the dog away, holding him around the neck.

"Settle that dog down, now. You've got work to do. I'm setting up an exercise routine for you, and with your brothers' help, you're going to carry it on after I leave." He swatted irritably at LeRoy who came sniffing on up to him.

"Task number one: pull-ups. I'll demonstrate."

Stanley grasped the T end of the laundry line, bent his legs so he was dangling with straight arms, and pulled himself up until his chin was above the bar.

"There," he said, red faced and puffing as he

dropped to a crouch. "That's a pull-up. Hey, enough with the licking! Someone hold the dog. All right then, who's next?"

Matthew called first, but it was immediately clear that the Bigs would bend the laundry poles clear out of the ground, so it was Little Klein's turn. It looked easy enough, and if his dad could pull his big self up, Little Klein imagined how easy it would be to raise his small self. He gave LeRoy's ears a quick scratch, then stepped out.

Luke lifted him to the bar, then let go. Little Klein lost his grip and fell to the ground. LeRoy was all over him, licking his face and whimpering.

"Get the dog out of the way," Stanley insisted. Mark held LeRoy back. Luke lifted Little Klein again and let go more gently this time. He dangled, his fingers growing red and sweaty on the bar. He pulled. He heaved. Little Klein toiled under the weight he didn't know he owned until his slippery hands betrayed him and he crumpled on the grass.

Everyone looked down on him in silence as LeRoy bathed his face again. These were boys and a man who'd never known weakness. From the day they stepped out of their cradles, they'd not given strength a thought. Strength, like height and girth, simply was—like eye color or curly hair. So this boy whose arms would not lift the rest of the body was an inexplicable curiosity to them. A mystery. As he caught up on his breath, Little Klein grasped a handful of the long and tangled hair he refused to get cut. He'd read the story of Sampson and his strength-giving hair, but it certainly didn't seem to be giving Little Klein any advantages.

"How about push-ups?" suggested Mark. "Push-ups would help him do pull-ups."

"That's thinking," said Stanley Klein.

All three boys and Stanley lay on the ground under the laundry line, then one by one demonstrated the proper form for Little Klein. When it was his turn, Little Klein's belly would not leave the grass. LeRoy lay down on all four paws and barked.

"Sit-ups would make his stomach stronger for lifting himself in push-ups," suggested Luke.

"Good idea," agreed their dad.

Again, demonstrations followed. This time it was Little Klein's back that would not give up its resting place.

"Maybe if he didn't sit in the tree all the time," Matthew said. "Maybe if he walked around more, his whole body would get stronger and he could do all of these things."

Little Klein stood and went to his tree. He climbed up halfway.

"This takes strength," he said. "None of the other guys can do this."

"That's because we're too big," Matthew answered. "Dad, he hardly has to walk anywhere. He gets to catch a ride on the bike or go piggyback all the time. Mother doesn't think he should get worn down."

Stanley stood up and brushed off his pants.

"Let me think," he said. Truthfully, with no results to inspire him, he was already losing interest in this project.

"You're absolutely right, Matthew. Little Klein," he called up to the tree, "I'm going in to talk to your mother. You're going to start with basic conditioning, and by that I mean getting around on your own two flippers, duckling. Got it?"

Little Klein nodded and climbed higher than he ever had before, so high he could see clear over his own roof and three streets beyond to the station, where a train would take his father away again the next morning.

A Magician's
Bag of Tricks

Harold was recognized as part of the Klein Boys when he was with his brothers, but on his own he was anonymous. His chin did not clear the counter at Gamble's Hardware, and he often lost his place in the line at Candy's Candies when people overlooked him.

Since the Minister incident, Mother Klein worried about Little Klein being pulled into the river by a hooked fish and drowning. While she had not exactly forbidden him to go angling with his brothers, she had managed every time to find some reason he had to stay behind. The garden needed weeding and watering. The floors needed dusting and he was the only one who could get all the way under the davenport.

One day with two quarters in his pocket to buy stamps, Little Klein and LeRoy took the long way to the Lena post office, past the Skelly gas station. On a bench outside the station door, Mr. Holt and Mr. Cutter were muttering over their checkers game. When Mr. Cutter won, as always, Little Klein took LeRoy inside to inquire after any current money-making ventures. Sam was busy with a customer, so he pulled a stool up to the counter and studied the customer's son, who was fiddling with a deck of cards.

"Pick a card," the boy said to Little Klein. Little Klein pulled a two of spades.

"Two of spades," said the boy.

"Lucky guess," said Little Klein. "Let me try again."

"King of diamonds."

"Did you shuffle?"

"Sure, watch. Now pull another one."

Little Klein consulted LeRoy. "Sniff this, boy. Whaddya think?"

"Hey, humans only!" the boy protested.

Little Klein held his hand over the deck, studying the boy's eyes as he drew a card.

"Ace of hearts," pronounced the magician.

"How do you do that?"

"Magic," said the boy as he walked out the door with his father.

"Did you see that?" Little Klein asked Sam.

"It's just a trick. Anyone can learn tricks," said Sam. "Don't have chores for you today, buddy. The shelves are all dusted and no deliveries till later in the week. Sorry." He reached under the counter, then tossed a dog biscuit to LeRoy.

"That's okay," said Little Klein glumly. As he walked, he imagined himself pulling the card trick on his brothers.

"How'd you do that?" they'd ask in amazement.

"Magic," he'd say with a modest shrug. His brothers would bring him along to perform for their friends.

"How'd he do that?" they'd ask in hushed voices.

"Magic," the Bigs would say as Little Klein pulled a quarter from behind Lucy McCrea's ear.

When school started back in the fall, the kids would gather around him at recess while he showed off a new trick. Instead of Twig, they'd call him Whiz or Shark or Sly. The Bigs would be known as Sly's brothers.

Gamble's Hardware was next to the post office. Little Klein told LeRoy to stay and wrestled with the temptation to open the door. He was supposed to go to the post office, buy fifteen stamps with the quarters, and then go straight home with a nickel change. Having already detoured past the filling station, he knew he should move on.

"Excuse me," said a teenager, reaching over his head. Little Klein was swept into the store in front of her floating dress, and once inside, there was nothing to do but walk past the toy shelves. There were model airplanes and Slinkies and the small statue of a bird he'd long admired. There was a Betsy Wetsy doll he'd often puzzled over and wished to see demonstrated. There were decks of cards, but he was sure not just any ordinary deck of cards could release his inner magician.

Then, next to a discounted copy of *The Poky Little Puppy*, he saw it. *A Magician's Bag of Tricks* was a fetching drawstring bag with a tiny book tied to the string. Little Klein took it reverently off the shelf and sat down on the floor to study it. Forty-nine cents. He would never come up with forty-nine cents all at once. He felt the bumpy sack, wondering at its contents. In his concentration he did not hear the voices at the counter.

"Come on, Mildred. It's dead in here. Lock up for a bit and let's go have lunch. Clara shops in your dad's store. You should support her lunch counter." Thus persuaded, Mildred turned over the OPEN sign in the door and added a note next to CLOSED that read FOR JUST A BIT.

Back in the toy department, Little Klein was desperately trying to rethread the drawstring through its little tunnel after it'd snapped when he'd given the knot a tug. His face burned and his stomach churned. Mildred Gamble had forbidden the Big Kleins from entering the store after a misguided elbow had cleared a shelf of imitation crystal whatnots she'd ordered especially for Valentine's Day. She'd hoped Sam would notice the swan and, knowing how much she adored swans, would slip in and buy it on her day off. Then, with just one day until Valentine's, it was a pile of shards on the floor. The ensuing commotion had roused her father from the nails and screws section and instead of supporting her banishment of those brutish Kleins, he'd admonished her—*her!*—for having ordered such nonsense in the first place.

"People can go down to Wanda's if they want dust-magnet trinkets," he'd lectured as she swept.

Little Klein had ducked out unnoticed that day, but he was sure that even if Mildred didn't recognize him, damaging her stock would end his browsing privileges permanently. Mildred Gamble had an eagle eye for mischief.

The need to relieve himself was suddenly urgent. He tiptoed to the back of the store. Maybe if he left the magic kit behind the wastebasket in the restroom, she wouldn't notice it for a few days. The basket was nearly empty now so it could even be a week before it got taken out. His problem solved, Little Klein stepped confidently back into the store and walked up the side aisle, planning to slip nonchalantly out the front door.

He wiped his sweaty palms on his pants as he neared the door and without looking at the counter pulled hard. It didn't budge. Panicking now, he pulled again, and again it stuck. He glanced over his shoulder, but Mildred was not at the counter. He turned around slowly.

"Hello?" he called in a thin voice. "Hello?"

Only the clock answered with its monotone tick. He looked out the window at LeRoy sniffing hopefully around customers coming out of the bakery and replayed the scene in his mind. He'd walked in the store. The door was open then. Mildred had been at the counter. He'd walked to the toy section. He'd heard Mildred talking to the girl who'd pushed him in the door. He'd found the magic bag. He'd heard Mildred laughing. After that he couldn't remember hearing her again. He'd shaken the bag, squished its mysterious contents, then pulled at the drawstring until it snapped. He'd been chanting *abracadabra* to himself just for practice.

That was it.

Little Klein had made Mildred and her friend disappear.

He ran back to the bathroom and grabbed the magic kit. There was no turning back now. He spread the contents out on the floor: a deck of cards, three stacking cups, a silky red scarf, a fake mustache. He tore the book from the string. If he didn't get Mildred back, he'd never see another allowance as long as he lived.

Little Klein opened the *Magician's Bag of Tricks* manual, hoping for a quick solution. He turned pages looking for pictures, but the small drawings showed him nothing to solve his problem. He went back to the first page and started reading. As he reached the top of page three, "Tools of the Trade," the front door jangled open.

"Watch the counter while I go do my lipstick," came Mildred's voice, followed by the clicking of her heels. Little Klein scrambled to his feet, and when the bathroom door swung open, Mildred screamed to find a boy inside. Little Klein stepped backward and heard a crunch. They both looked down. Splinters of three stacking cups surrounded Little Klein's foot. Mildred put her hands on her hips and snapped her gum.

"You break it, you buy it," she ordered.

Little Klein just stared at her.

"You reappeared," he whispered.

"Yeah. Magic," she said. "What's your name? Were you hiding in here while I was gone? Did you take anything else? You better pay for that or I'll have to call my dad in and he'll either call your mother or the cops. Depends what kind of mood he's in." She stooped to pick up the empty red bag. "Forty-nine cents. Cough it up."

Mildred's friend had run back when she heard the scream. She watched as the small, pale boy dug in his pocket and pulled out two quarters.

"Now get out of here," Mildred directed, pointing toward the front door. Little Klein did not need an invitation. He shoved the magic bag in his pocket, whistled for LeRoy, and ran. They were a block from home before he remembered about the stamps. If only he'd gotten to read far enough to find out about pulling coins from the backs of ears.

Castle

LeRoy cried at the moon. He'd found his family. He'd taken care of them. He'd herded his boys to the river and back and kept them out of trouble. When the back door swung open every morning, LeRoy popped out of his house and stood at attention to see what would happen next and what would be expected of him, but nothing was expected of him and that was the trouble. He'd protected his family from raccoons, cats, postal delivery, milk delivery, and every other manner of intrusion, but they went on as if cats and raccoons didn't exist and approaching people were friends.

All summer he'd found shelter in the little guardhouse his boys had built for him. While sleeping between walls and under the same roof every night was new and not so pleasing to LeRoy, he didn't want to insult his boys. He had to be careful on entering and turning around in his house as there were nails poking through the walls. One summer day melted into the next and boredom overtook LeRoy. He lost interest in chasing and grew heavy with lazy napping.

Then in August the Bigs left town to work on the Filmore Farm. One day Little Klein was left home alone, and he invited LeRoy to come inside the big house. The treasures stored in the castle were beyond LeRoy's imagination.

"Here, boy," Little Klein said. "This is the kitchen. This is where humans eat." He set a plate on the table. "We put our dishes on a table. See? And we sit in chairs."

LeRoy panted. He followed his snout around the kitchen. The bouquet! And the feast on the floor! Treats in all the corners—oatmeal clumps, bread crumbs, cheese. Little Klein put a sandwich on his plate and sat at the table. He took a bite and looked at LeRoy, who stood guard at his side.

"Want some, boy?"

LeRoy barked.

Little Klein tore off a piece of bread and dropped it for LeRoy.

"Woof!" He looked up at the boy, hoping to play the game again.

"You should try eating like us," said Little Klein. "Think you can do it?" He got another plate and put it at the place next to his and pulled out the chair.

"Here, boy. Sit here."

LeRoy leaped up onto the chair, his front paws sprawling onto the table, sending Little Klein's plate skittering, but not before he snatched the sandwich off of it.

"No, boy! No! You aren't supposed to take anyone else's food. This is your plate. See? LeRoy's plate. Let's try again."

LeRoy ate bread and cheese until even the trash can didn't smell appetizing. Then Little Klein gave him a tour of the rest of the house.

Each room had its own scent. In the living room was a davenport softer than any bed of needles, and LeRoy settled in for a nap.

"No, boy! Get off! You're leaving hairs everywhere!" Little Klein shooed LeRoy off the couch and swiped his arm across the spot where he'd been lying.

The bathroom offered a bowl of fragrant water—an indoor pond! Little Klein pressed a lever, and the water drained, then reappeared. LeRoy barked.

A dry powdery smell filled Mother Klein's room, which LeRoy toured quietly. Then he galloped up the stairs after Little Klein to the best room of all. Here lived dirty clothes, wet towels, a cookie. And on the bed, pillowcases ripe with the individual scent of each of his boys' hair and drool. LeRoy yelped for joy.

Just when he had forgotten that the outside world existed, Little Klein called him.

"That's it, boy. You've gotta get back outside before Mother gets home."

LeRoy hung his head and followed Little Klein to the yard.

After that day, LeRoy's doghouse felt unbearably small and cramped and devoid of aroma. He took up whining at the door whenever his family was inside. Perhaps they didn't really need him after all.

"What has gotten into that dog?" Mother Klein mused.

Recipe for Sleep

Alone now in the big upstairs, Little Klein's nightmares were unleashed. Wolves chased his trembling behind; boulders crushed his house while he slept; a big wind blew him away, and he couldn't grab hold of passing trees. While the Bigs were gone, Little Klein's nightmares played like horror marathon week at the Riverview Theater. He resisted bedtime because he didn't want to go to sleep, yet he didn't want to be the only one awake in the house, either. The room without the Bigs was a cavern.

Mother tried all her sleep remedies. She told him stories, sang him the spider song, fed him warm milk and butter bread. She let him sleep in one of his father's nightshirts because he liked the softness of it. But every night it was the same routine, Little Klein pestering her to stay awake so he could fall asleep.

"Why can't LeRoy sleep with me?" he pleaded, but the answer never changed.

"What if something happens to Matthew?" he worried. "Or Mark? Or Luke? Or all of them? Who will protect me then? What if they don't come home?"

Mother Klein dismissed his worries. "I don't worry about your brothers," she said, and sang through the hymnal by heart until he fell asleep. But the next night was the same. And the following.

"Would you read to me about cake?" called Little Klein from the bedroom one night. Mother Klein shrugged. "What do you mean?" she called back.

"I mean, will you read me about cake? You

know, crack an egg, one cup of flour, like that."

Mother pondered.

Though he was small for his age, Little Klein had the appetite of one of the Bigs. He was transfixed by the magic with which water and heat turned crisp dry oats into warm mush for breakfast and the way an unappetizing lump of raw eggs and flour and cocoa could turn into a cake with the texture of a spring meadow. Even the power of butter to fuse two pieces of bread together delighted Little Klein.

"Well, excitement is in the mind of the beholder," said Mother Klein. She pulled her worn cookbook off the shelf and opened it. "It's worth a try."

"What kind of cake?" she asked.

"Chocolate," said Little Klein, snuggling down into his blanket.

"Here goes. 'Best Chocolate Cake. Heat oven to three hundred and fifty degrees.'"

"No," said Little Klein, "start with the ingredients."

"What was I thinking? The ingredients: 'Two cups all-purpose flour or cake flour, two cups sugar, one teaspoon soda—'"

"What's soda?" Little Klein interrupted.

Mother Klein explained the ingredients as they went through the list. By the time she got to the happily ever after of "pour evenly into pan(s)," Little Klein was asleep, a peaceful smile on his face, a drop of drool edging out the side of his mouth.

Recipes worked for a few nights, first chocolate cake, then gingerbread, then anything with lots of ingredients and several steps. Soon, though, Little Klein's anticipation of nightmares was worse than the nightmares themselves, and his bedtime demands got more complicated. Dessert was no longer enough. He needed a main dish first, then a salad course, and a song after dessert. When he asked Mother Klein one night to read him a breakfast, lunch, and dinner, she snapped shut her *Joy of Cooking* and stood up.

"Enough," she said. "My bedtime services

from now on will include one song and a prayer. Now, go get your dog. If there are any nightmares lurking, his smell will surely keep them at bay."

By the time the Bigs returned from the farm, chipmunks had taken up residence in the doghouse and LeRoy, like Goldilocks, had tried out each of their beds, sleeping every night, though, with Little Klein.

Paws on the Windowsill

Night after night LeRoy patrolled the long and narrow upstairs bedroom. Sometimes he needed the benefit of a tree so badly and his boys slept so soundly that he had to wake Mother Klein to be let out. But that was his only complaint.

One night after his tree run, LeRoy peeked over the edge of Little Klein's bed to make sure he was asleep. Then he pattered between the other three beds, sniffing at still feet and damp hair, and under beds for remnants of sandwiches or crackers. He nearly woke Mark when he got into a chase with what turned out to be a bunny of dust, which, once caught, made him sneeze. These were now LeRoy's nightly rounds, and he trotted proudly, then, paws up on the window-sill, looked out at the moon, a howl building in his belly. He gave it just a small hollow voice, though, lest he be sent outside for the rest of the night.

He crawled up on Little Klein's feet and laid down his head. Now that LeRoy slept indoors, truth was he'd grown skittish about the out-doors after dark. It was a good thing Little Klein needed protection from bad dreams.

The next day toward evening, the boys walked to the town park for a game of baseball. There were lots of kids around, and LeRoy was not the only dog. The struggle to keep track of his boy in the crowd put LeRoy in an irascible mood, and when he found Little Klein hunched down petting some puff of a pup, he couldn't help himself—he barked so loud the puppy wet the ground right there, and then LeRoy nipped him.

"LeROY!" Little Klein gasped.

"Why, I never!" exclaimed Mildred Gamble, hardware store maven, swooping the puppy into her arms.

"Fluffy, are you hurt?"

LeRoy barked again, but his bravado wavered when he saw the look on his boy's face.

"You're mighty lucky Fluffy isn't hurt, young man," Mildred continued. "I ought to call the pound." She leaned down and gave LeRoy a swift slap on the snout. "Bad dog!"

LeRoy lunged to nip her, too, but an arm at his neck held him back and he watched the fluff ball disappear with Mildred Gamble while his boy talked soothingly into his ear. Then another brother was there holding out a piece of frankfurter, and LeRoy forgot all about being ornery. He pranced along between his boys the rest of the evening, running with them when the clouds turned suddenly dark and the rain started. When they got home, he barely paused at his doghouse, he'd grown so accustomed to slipping in the screen door behind his brood.

The rain kept LeRoy awake nearly till

morning, and when he did finally sleep, his dreams rumbled with the terror of lost boys, of muted barks, of swimming after a floating Fluffy, who in dream's translation was larger and fiercer than LeRoy.

Doghouse Down

The sky drained for days and by the time it paused, cabin fever was epidemic. An unbearable stillness hung over the town, a heat so soggy Little Klein's socks lay still damp by his bed in the morning. Then LeRoy woke them up early with his feet, sniffing and licking.

Little moaned about getting the smallest bowl of oatmeal, and all three Bigs growled at him to Shut Up.

"That's it," declared Mother Klein, whapping the wooden spoon against the counter with a snap that broke it in two and made the boys jump. "It's too hot in here for the five of us. I've been cooped up in this house too long with your bickering and wrestling and . . . and . . . et cetera. I want you all outside doing something constructive. Preferably out of my sight."

Little Klein couldn't believe she was including him in the decree. "Yes," she added, "you, too. Clear your dishes and get."

They stumbled out the back door and sat on the steps.

"Hey, make room for me," complained Little Klein.

Luke pushed Mark off the end and scooted over. Just as Little sat, Mark got up and shoved back, bumping Luke into Little, who smashed into Matthew, who got up and raised his arm at the whole mess of them.

Mother Klein came to the door. "Either find a task or I'll find one for you." She tossed their shoes out after them.

Little Klein slouched over to LeRoy's doghouse and picked at a loose shingle on the edge of the roof. Matthew swooped him up and tossed him over the doghouse to Luke.

"Hey! Stop that! Put me down!"

"Sure. Here you go," and with that Little Klein was deposited on the roof of the doghouse. He slid down slanted boards to the ground. It was kind of fun.

"Hey, do it again!" Once again Luke hoisted his brother to the roof for a bumpy slide to the ground.

"My turn," said Mark and Matthew at once, and they dived at the roof from opposite sides, colliding in a heap over the top.

"Make room!" shouted Luke, who piled on top of the other two. Little Klein tried to join the pileup by climbing the dangling legs.

"I'm suffocating under here," called the bottom Klein, and when the pile shifted there was a slow crack, then a snap, and before the sounds registered in their brains as breaking boards, the sloped roof flattened, then collapsed, and four heads and torsos were trapped inside the buckling walls.

The Klein boys sorted out their limbs and rose slowly to their feet.

"Sliver!" Little Klein yanked at a small splinter of wood stuck in his hand.

"Look at all the nails," Luke said. They stepped back gingerly and stood in shocked silence around the wreckage.

Mother Klein came to the door and sighed. Then she shook her head and went back inside, taking LeRoy with her.

Outside, Little Klein broke the silence. "Luke ruined LeRoy's doghouse."

"You started it, squirt."

"Did not!"

"Did too!"

"Now what are we going to do?" asked Mark.

"You're all a bunch of sissies," Matthew scoffed.

Glares were passed around. Little Klein stepped forward and pulled a loose board off the side of the doghouse and laid it on the ground. He yanked off another and set it neatly next to the first one. "Now LeRoy's got a window," he said.

But soon the window turned into a door and then the wall was lost all together, the house now beyond saving as one loose board led to another. While his brothers took over the dismantling, Little Klein darted around them, picking up boards and sorting out the splintered ones from the good ones.

"Here," he said, tossing a shingle to Matthew, who started a pile. Mark picked through the wreckage for nails. Luke walked around Little Klein's boards.

"Look at this," he said, pointing to the neat rows. "What do you see?"

They all stood up and stared. "What?"

"We have enough wood here to build a raft!"

"I was thinking about a tree house . . ." started Little Klein. But his voice was drowned out by the excitement of the Bigs, who were already planning a raft. Then Little Klein saw himself on the raft, floating along the middle of the river. He saw himself passing right over the den of The Minister and reaching down to scoop him up with a net. He abandoned his plans and joined his brothers. "Go look in the garage for rope," commanded Matthew.

"And see if you can find a tarp in the basement," added Luke.

Mother Klein brought out a basket with sandwiches and bottles of milk as they finished their raft.

"Have a picnic by the river," she said. "And don't take Wilson's Fork."

"We know, Ma."

"Keep an eye on the sky. I don't trust this hot, still air. And be back for dinner," she added.

"We know."

LeRoy barked at the door, and Mother Klein let him out.

"Wait for LeRoy!" she called unnecessarily as LeRoy bounded out, yapping and trying to get his nose in the basket.

"And keep track of your brother; he's not a strong swimmer."

"*We know,*" said the Bigs as Little Klein moaned, "Mother!"

The Falls

The Klein Boys balanced their craft on the back of Mark's bike and pushed it out of town. LeRoy followed them to the river, where Little Klein launched his brothers into the porcelain water with a shove that left him on shore.

"Wait for me!" he cried as a swirling current caught the raft on its conveyor belt. The Big Kleins were spinning; they were sailing fast.

"No fair!" Little Klein stomped as the raft rounded the bend.

"Wrong way!" he yelled when it turned at the river's fork. LeRoy nudged Little Klein. He barked and ran up the bank. He turned and barked again.

"Shoot, LeRoy. We get left behind again." Little Klein scrambled through the raspberry bushes after LeRoy. He heard yelling. Little Klein ran faster, trying to follow LeRoy's barks. Mother was going to be so mad they'd taken Wilson's Fork. They may have taken off without him, but at least he wouldn't get in trouble. At the top of the bank he saw the raft again, and his smug heart went limp. The raft was stuck on a rock in the middle of the river, but there were no Kleins on board. LeRoy was already in the water, swimming instinctively now as in his dreams to the three heads that popped up, a constellation in the river's thundering sky.

"Help!" screamed Mark.

"Shoot!" called Luke.

"The falls!" cried Matthew as he latched onto the dog.

The falls.

Little Klein ran for the road. He ran and yelled, stumbled and yelled.

"Help! Help! Help!"

By the time he reached the road his voice was no thicker than kite string and the passing car was moving too fast to notice a small boy in the brush. A thicket of brambles caught Little Klein. He yanked one leg then the other, wrestling himself free before stepping onto the tar shoulder. He could see a silhouette across the two-lane, but was it human or animal?

"Help!" he gasped, but the shape did not move. He pursed his lips, but he was out of whistle, too. He shivered like January, teeth rattling, kneecaps quaking. Little Klein put his two index fingers in his mouth, Rich Wedge's method, and he blew. Nothing. He spat. He stomped. He licked his lips, puckered, and tried again. This time—Oh, Glory Halleluia—his instrument trilled; it trumpeted. The shadow quivered and rose.

Holy Moses, it was Mean Emma Brown. He sucked in his breath. One strip of tar separated him from the boy-squasher. If it weren't that Little Klein needed the Big Kleins to protect him from Emma Brown in all the futures he hoped to have, he would have backed away. But now she had seen him.

She tramped her big brown boots across both lanes without looking for cars. She laced her big brown fingers together and cracked her bony knuckles. When the bellow of Emma's "*What?*" hit Little Klein, his bladder released.

"The falls!" he whimpered.

"I can see that," Emma snorted. "You call me over here for a square of toilet paper?"

Now Little Klein's eyes released, too. "My brothers!"

Emma looked hard at Little Klein. "Your brothers aren't . . . they didn't . . . Wilson's Fork?"

Little Klein nodded.

"Aw, crap!" said Emma. "I'd just about caught a dragonfly over there. Crap. Well, step on out."

Little Klein looked at her wide.

"You stand in that lane; I'll stand in this one," she continued. "Try to look tall."

Little Klein stood on the yellow line, his

legs wet and sticky, snot running over the bridge of his quivering lip. He drew a hot raspy breath and raised his shoulders as far as he could.

Little Klein thought about his futures. There was his air hero future. He was a member of Captain Midnight's Secret Squadron and had in his damp pocket at this moment his Photomatic Code-O-Graph. When Captain Midnight's eyesight got bad, as it was sure to searching for Ivan Shark in the dark, Little Klein would be ready to take over.

There was his farmer future, where he rode a horse that made him taller than all the other Kleins and where he had a pack of wolves that bared their teeth should Mean Emma Brown even think about stealing corn from his field.

Little Klein slid one eye in Emma's direction. Soon his brothers would be here to raise their fists at her. His brothers must have climbed out of the river by now. They were probably sneaking up behind Emma, laughing as they plotted their surprise attack.

Then there was his golden future. The future that featured Little Klein as a star boxer, raising his dukes to the likes of Joe Louis and Sugar Ray Robinson. He'd have red silk shorts and brown leather gloves the size of balloons. From town to town he'd ride in his very own pickup truck, with all the banana sandwiches he could eat in a cooler on the seat next to him. There would be photos of Little Klein in the drugstores. Little scrappers would ask for his autograph.

In each of Little Klein's futures there were Big Kleins. Big Kleins filling the tank of his fighter plane. Big Kleins driving plows through his fields. Big Kleins collecting bets before fights and clearing his path through the cheering crowds. Soon Big Kleins would be grabbing him off this hot pavement and leaving him stranded in a high tree or dangling him over the rushing river from a hanging branch.

The rushing river.

The road was deserted.

After a thousand years a pickup sputtered around the bend, tooted its horn, and coasted onto the shoulder next to Emma. An ancient woman leaned out the window.

"What's a matter, girl?"

Emma pointed at Little Klein.

"The Klein Boys're caught a current."

"Fool boys, in the river after those rains," Nora Nettle scoffed. "Hop in the back."

Emma grabbed Little Klein and hoisted him into a heap of rope and barrels and fishing rods, then climbed in herself. The truck lurched forward and off the road, bumping and scraping through the brush until it skidded to a stop at the edge of the falls. Emma and Nora Nettle climbed out to the cliff. Little Klein, caught in a tangle of rope and fishing line, hollered for his brothers.

"Come on out, guys!" he shouted. "I got her cornered!" He wrestled himself free and dropped over the edge of the truck. No sweaty hand grabbed his puny arm. No smelly breath hissed a snake scare in his ear. No sweeping arm lifted him off his feet. Little Klein stomped around the side of the truck.

"Guys!" he shouted. "Come on, guys!" Little Klein wiped his hand across his eyes and let out a roar.

"Stop it, you guys!"

A shivering blanket of wet fur yelped at Little Klein's side. "LeRoy!" he cried. "Good boy, LeRoy. You swam, LeRoy! Good boy! Where are the guys, LeRoy?" He wrapped his arms around the dog's neck. "You're okay, boy. Shake it out, shake it out, come on, shake off all that water!" Little Klein shook himself all over to demonstrate. LeRoy gave a little shake and laid his head on his paws.

Then Emma was standing next to him. Mean Emma Brown was looking at him with her railroad nail eyes.

Little Klein bared his teeth at Emma Brown and put up his dukes. "Where're my brothers?"

Emma looked into Little Klein's eyes, into all his pasts and all his futures. She lifted Little Klein back into the nest of rope and fishing line. Then she dropped the shaking dog into his lap and got into the cab with Nora Nettle.

"Wait!" cried Little Klein. "My mother will kill me if I come home without the boys!"

The wheels spun in the wet sand then caught their tread on the dirt and the truck lumbered back through the brush, back up the hill, back onto the hot, deserted tar.

The River

The river did not intend to swallow people. New waters flowed by the town of Lena every day on their predestined journey. Every day new waters were discovering the quiet green shores, the soaring bluffs, and the rocky and sandy bottom that adorned this particular part of their passage. Here, the river narrowed and widened, rounded bends and skirted boulder beds, then split for a ways into two branches—one calm and even, the other sending the water tumbling over a cliff in a joyful free fall.

Long before the river was born, a warm ocean covered this part of the continent. When the water of the ancient ocean disappeared, it left sediment piled so high in one place that when the rest of the area got locked in glaciers, this plateau was missed, a rocky island alone for thousands of years in a frozen sea. Sliced top to bottom, this plateau would look like a many-layered rock cake topped with limestone.

Future children would easily carve their initials with sticks in this soft stone, and when melting glaciers to the north birthed the river, its waters had no trouble cutting through it. So easily did the limestone dissolve, in fact, that simple rain cracked its surface in places.

By the time the glaciers had disappeared and humans lived on the land, eroding water had carved out caves, caverns, and underground rivers from the limestone. Even this river, intent on its mission to feed larger water bodies, was unaware of the vast geography of its buried sister streams and only during floods did it explore the caves.

The waters that passed each season were new, but they were related by the continuous cycle of drops pulled out of the ocean into the air and dropped back down by heavy clouds. Reincarnated sometimes in the very same river, they enjoyed the trip all the more the second time through, like revisiting a childhood home and finding it smaller than one remembers.

The waters that flowed past Lena after heavy rains were the most unpredictable waters. They had a nervous disposition and were easily rallied into tight spinning currents with magnetic grips. Farther down their journey they would look back on that portion of the trip with a sigh—oh, the exuberance of youth—for Lena was only a day's journey from the birthplace of the river. And like impetuous youth, the early waters sometimes acted without regard for consequence.

That's how it had been two years ago when a celebratory group took a trip on her surface. They intended to put in at Lena proper and disembark at the park near the river's fork for the annual First Picnic of the Year in which the music of the falling river in the distance would be their entertainment.

That spring the waters flowed quietly past Lena proper. It wasn't until just before the fork that the waters gathered together in a magnetic twirl, ready to dance and fly off the cliff together. With some of the youngest and oldest citizens of the town standing onshore, the waters of that spring carried the long boat on their current past the park, past the food and streamers and horseshoes, and didn't release it until it was airborne.

As the water found its path again below the cliff, it coughed up wood and shoes and Felicia Olson and Crumly Bottom and Lester Prentice and Floyd Ranborn and the Brown couple and many more. Some the water left by banks and in weeds; others it carried on before Officer Linden and his crew lifted them out.

Now the river was running high again. Heavy rains had added a powerful depth to the river that was disguised near town by a serene skin. When three boys on a slatted raft grazed its surface, the river's dark memory trembled. The waters for whom this was a return journey knew the falls were ahead. Even as they pulled the raft into Wilson's Fork, they knew the fate of these boys and steered the craft onto a jutting rock. But the raft met the rock too fast, and the boys could not hold on. The river was able to release their dog into a clump of weeds and brush, but not the boys. The current pulled them in, pulled them down, swallowed those boys whole as it skimmed toward the cliff.

Terrified at its own strength, the water below the falls caught the boys and held them in a churning grip, churning but not sending them downriver. Finally, the river tucked those boys, one by one, safely into a chamber of ancient rock bed worn into a cave by generations of river water. Only a shoe and a cap were released to travel on farther.

Missing

Bumping along in the back of the Nora Nettle's pickup truck put the ice of a nightmare in Little Klein's chest. His nightmares all had one thing in common. Whether he was facing a pack of wolves or arriving at school in his underwear, he was alone. In his nightmares no one called him Little Klein because there were no Big Kleins in Harold's nightmares.

It was only LeRoy's slobber on his foot that assured him now in this truck that he wasn't dreaming. Harold Sylvester George Klein grabbed LeRoy's face and lifted it to look at him.

"LeRoy. You've got to help me find the guys."

LeRoy whimpered and laid his head back down.

The rickety truck bounced slowly along.

"What if they're drowning, LeRoy? What if they're calling for help? Why can't she go faster?" he pleaded in vain. All the cold fright turned to hot rage in Harold's chest as he relived the moment the raft had slipped out of his reach.

"They left me on shore!" He pounded his fist on the barrel next to him.

"Ouch!"

"They left me on SHORE! They ditched me. Again! Bullies. We're going back. Come on."

Harold braced his feet against LeRoy's side and pushed until the dog slid toward the end of the truck. He scooted his rear forward and pushed again until they were at the gate. He looked back at the cab, but the window was too dirty for him to see in or for Emma to see out. The gate latch had been eaten by rust and just a rope looped over a hook held it closed. Once released, the gate flopped down like a slide to the tar slowly rolling out below them.

"Ready, LeRoy?"

LeRoy whimpered and laid his head on his paws, looking up at Harold with what he hoped was his most pitiful gaze but which Harold interpreted as a nod of agreement.

"Good boy. There's my boy. This old truck is barely moving. It'll be easy. Close your eyes. I'll count. One . . . two . . . three!" Harold pushed off and slid out of the truck, landing with a thud that knocked the wind out of him.

"See," he said when he caught his breath. "Nothing broken. That wasn't so bad, was it, boy? LeRoy?"

The road next to him was empty. Turning, he saw LeRoy's face in the truck bed, growing small. His mouth was open in a bark, but the sound was lost in the rattle of the pickup.

"Shoot, LeRoy!" Harold stood up. "Ow! Ow! Ow!" He tested out his limbs. Everything worked, but his sitter smarted with every step. "I'm going to get those guys," he muttered as he trudged along. As soon as he started feeling sorry for himself, his energy waned. So Harold mustered up all the old grudges stored in that little-used part of his heart.

"Can't even get a dumb old dog to follow me." He walked a little faster as he mimicked the deeper voices of his brothers. "Little Klein isn't big enough to ride a bike. Little Klein isn't strong enough to fly a kite. Little Klein isn't tall enough to . . . Three milk shakes and oh, a strawberry kiddie cone for him." Harold kicked a stone. "I want vanilla!" he screamed at the top of his lungs. "In fact, forget the cone—I want a root beer float!" He started to jog.

"Gardens are not just for sissies!" He clenched his fists.

"Ditchers!" A squirrel was rooting around on the side of the road. Harold hissed at him. "Scat, you!" he shouted.

Then he saw the tire tracks coming up out of the grass and leading into the trees. Harold stopped. He turned to follow the tracks.

"Be there, guys. Be there," he chanted in a

whisper with each step. The sweat that had drenched him while he ran returned as an uncomfortable chill when he reached the dense shade of the trees. All his blood huddled in his heart, thumping and pumping, threatening to burst out of his chest. His feet heavy and his head light, Little Klein followed the sound of the falls until he was standing at the edge of the cliff. He whistled, then stopped to listen. Nothing.

Had Mean Emma Brown and the old lady seen something and not told him? He didn't see any dead bodies on the shore or floating in the water. Just a lone board, caught going round and round where the falls hit the river below.

"Come on out! I won't tell!" he shouted, then whistled again, but the falling water drowned out even his whistle. He ran his hands over the goose bumps on his arms while picking his way along the shore, then wound back up over the hill, around the bend, until he could see flattened grass where they'd sat on the raft before launching it in the river.

"They started here," he said in a soft, quivering voice, pantomiming his shove. He followed the path along the river again. "They started swirling there," he said a bit louder. He followed the trail over the hill where the river forked, then mustered his most determined voice: "And there's the rock that caught the raft."

Harold peered across the water. Had they gotten out on the other side? There was no movement. His calls brought no response. He looked over the falls again, and his knees melted. He knelt and looked downriver.

What if they did go over? He lay on his belly and pulled himself to the edge with his elbows until he was looking directly over the cliff, the spray of the water misting his face, the sound deadening his thoughts.

He covered his ears and tried to concentrate. What would happen if they did go over? The falls weren't so tall, not like Minnehaha Falls when he visited his aunties. Maybe the boys would go under at the bottom, but wouldn't they bob back up and float downstream? That had to be it. They must have crawled out where the river gets shallow and slow again. Emma Brown and the old lady just panicked when they didn't see them — that was all.

Harold pushed himself back from the edge and stood up. He walked through the woods to the place where a trail wound down the steep slope. Standing at the base of the falls, he looked up into the tower of water. He turned and started downriver, studying its surface and whistling into the woods. In one place the land rose above the river and Harold had to steel his squirming stomach and peer down again. Just beyond this was the footbridge.

He stood in the middle of the bridge and looked in both directions. It was when he kept following the river and looked back at the bridge that he saw it. Something caught on a reed under the bridge. He rushed back, splashing along the shore and wading carefully under the bridge. It was a black All-Star gym shoe. Size big.

"I knew it!" he exclaimed. "They're down

here somewhere." He left the shoe on the grass and searched for footprints, flattened grass, any sign of a herd of large, wet brothers. When clues eluded him and his whistles went unanswered, Harold finally dropped down, pulled his knees up to his chest, and wrapped his arms around them. No magic kit would make the Bigs reappear. For the first time in his life, Harold was alone, but he didn't feel small. It was his turn to take charge. The rhythm of a growing wind in the trees kept a steady beat in Harold's head, and with it the pulse of his problem. His brothers had gone over the falls. But they weren't in the river. Over the falls. Not in the river.

Harold stood up. The falls. He walked back.

He watched the sheets of water unfurl. Down they fell, down beneath the surface, then bubbling up again. If his brothers had gone under, would they bob up in front of the sheet or behind it?

What was behind the waterfall? He edged himself toward the wall, keeping his head down to avoid getting water in his eyes. Shielding his eyes with his hand, he peered behind the sheet of water. It wasn't a flat wall of rock as he'd imagined. It was pitted and creviced. Just above knee level was a shelf wide enough for a boy his size to climb on. Harold held his breath and stepped. To his surprise he did not slip into the grip of the water. He held on to a jutting rock next to him and breathed.

"Okay," he said out loud, preparing to step back to dry ground. "They're not here." But Harold's legs were more afraid than he was. They refused to budge.

"Holy Moses," he gasped. "Holy Moses and a can of nuts."

King

The name LeRoy means "king," and while LeRoy didn't know that, he had always fancied himself a fierce, fearless leader. He felt the admiration of his family, his subjects, and knew they'd follow his decrees. In his wandering days, he'd sauntered around with his tail in the air, a snarl at the ready, never following the other dogs.

But every creature holds at least one secret, and the day LeRoy watched Little Klein disappear on the pavement behind the pickup, LeRoy learned the truth about himself. LeRoy was a chipmunk in the body of a wolf.

Yes, his family answered his barks, but if they'd raised a hand at him, he'd have whimpered and hid. Sure he'd snarled, but only at dogs on leashes or behind fences. In his wandering days, when other wanderers, having finished their scraps at the back door of the bar, ran off in a pack, LeRoy always went in the opposite direction as if he'd had somewhere better to go, when really he simply craved the safety of his little spot by the river.

And now. Now LeRoy craved nothing more than to sleep in an upstairs bed out of the heat and damp and away from raccoons and unpredictable cats. But he'd lost his boys.

So powerful was his shame that when the truck rolled up to a stop sign in town, LeRoy jumped out and slunk between two garages. He curled up between a stack of firewood and a garbage can and closed his eyes.

His boys had been laughing. They were spinning. Then they were screaming.

LeRoy, who was scared of the fish in the river, had leaped in, hadn't he? He who had never stayed afloat had motored with all fours. But they kept disappearing. One head here, another there, then gone, then another scream. The water was pushing him. He'd paddled out. He'd crawled up the bank, and when he looked back, the heads weren't there.

Where were his boys? LeRoy tried to go to sleep, but the air was so empty of boy smell. He sniffed at the garbage can, but it was no good. He needed his boys. LeRoy rose up on his sturdy legs and picked his way to the alley and slouched slowly out of town.

As whiffs of bacon and oil gave way to sweet roadside clover and last week's angry skunk, LeRoy moved from his usual wander pace to a saunter. A building wind was roughing up his coat and confusing his nose.

LeRoy didn't used to have so many worries. Were there eight smelly shoes next to the back door at night? Was his pack together? Had one strayed? They were hard to herd, hard to herd.

Used to be LeRoy had few cares. Find some food. Find some shade. Find some tomfoolery.

Sleep. Life *was* simpler then. He used to have running dreams, before his family. Now he had chasing dreams, dreams of failed rescues, boys-in-danger dreams, dreams that he had no teeth and his legs were short like a house dog's and his tail ineffective like a cat's. Once he even dreamed he was a cat. LeRoy could, right this windy minute, crawl into the arms of some well-worn tree roots. But before he could muster the courage to quit, a gust of wind blew his tail clear off course and LeRoy imagined his littlest boy out there somewhere, unanchored.

Wind, trouble, boys. Wind, trouble, boys. LeRoy had a hunch. He joined forces with the wind, and LeRoy ran.

Then a car sped down the road toward LeRoy, and he skittered into the brush, catching himself up in a nasty tangle of dead nettles. The boys would pick him out of this mess. Where were his boys? The river. The river.

Deepest, Maddest, Biggest

Harold was a rattling bag of tinder sticks. *So this,* he thought as he tried to distract his feet and hands from the enormity of their current responsibilities, *is what Buster Ludlow meant when he said, "Get a sandwich, Kleinlet."* Maybe a few extra sandwiches would have padded him against these aggressive rocks poking into his ribs. The Bigs sure had padding enough. What would the Bigs do in his situation? One, they would find him and take him home before Mother knew he was missing. That's what Harold would do. He'd find the boys before

Mother knew anything had happened. That Mean Emma Brown was already on her way to spread panic. Harold was still paralyzed, but he could start by calling for his brothers.

"Guys!" he squeaked, and was immediately ashamed of the effort. "Guys!" he tried again. Harold thought about the wolf with those pigs and their houses. He'd need lungs like that wolf's. Harold reached down to his deepest growl, to his maddest memories, to his biggest thoughts. He drew in his widest breath, and Harold whistled.

The force of his effort swept him off his feet, and he landed with a *thwap* on his knees on the ledge, scraping his face on the way down. His nose pressed against the cool wall, he breathed in the dank air and tasted blood from his lip mixing with the bitter tang of the stone. He turned and shifted to his bum. In this position his feet found another perch just below. Harold hung his head. He put fingers around his smarting knees. Salty water leaked out the sides of his eyes. What was the use?

But he whistled again.

"Help!" came a shallow cry.

Harold didn't lift his head. "What?" he said sullenly.

"Help!" came the cry again.

Harold's head snapped up. Was he dreaming? He stood gingerly on the muddy lower ledge and shuffled farther from shore, to where the water surged out away from the ledge.

"Hello!" he shouted. "Guys? Guys? It's me! Hello?"

Silence.

Harold looked back at dry land. He looked out at the falling water. He slid ahead another foot before the ledge ended abruptly. Harold's stomach flipped. As he pondered his soupy death, there was another call.

"Help! We're down here!"

It was a Klein. And he sounded close— around-the-corner close.

"Where are you?"

"Here! Look down, look down!"

It was Mark's voice.

Harold's hands, already wet from the rocks, were now slick with sweat. If his heart hadn't already beat out of his chest, he was sure it would be popping through his T-shirt at any moment, probably busting open then and leaking all over his insides. What more damage could looking down do? Harold peered at the water churning below him, at the jutting rocks, at the height he'd managed to climb, and everything Harold had eaten in recent memory came up the elevator and launched itself out and down, down, down into the swirling mist.

Smells Like a Twister

A wind came up in Lena. A clothespin-popping, cat-launching, paper-delivering wind. It inhaled trees, drawing leaves and branches toward Market Road, then exhaled them like feather dusters wildly clearing the gathering clouds. Keen eyes, arthritic joints, and sharp olfactories were consulted to determine the nature and intent of this day's wind. Self-proclaimed experts gathered at Sam's Skelly, where Officer Linden presided, the warning lights and siren of his official vehicle at the ready.

"Sky's not green enough."

"It's too late in the season."

"Tornadoes are sidereal, and I seen no pre-diction in the stars last night."

"Stars? Hogwash. My knee remains one-hundred percent accurate, and it says we've got ourselves a tornado brewing."

"There's rotation in the clouds to the west."

"Nope, Harvey, them's straight-moving winds."

"S'not hot enough."

"Not humid 'nough either."

"Sure smells like a twister."

Widow Flom had been standing at the back of this town gathering, holding her tongue as if it were a wild puppy on a short leash. Finally, the leash snapped. "If I might add a modicum of actual science to this stew of nonsense, it's hotter than blazes, the sky is a wicked green, and these are no kite-flying winds. This looks to be a pernicious storm. Take your lame joints, starry eyes, and overgrown nozzles home where they belong. I can't believe I've stayed tuned this long."

The crowd erupted in indignation.

Officer Linden broke into the uproar. "Thank you, Mrs. Flom. Let's all just calm down here. Fact is we got ourselves a big wind. As usual, when it's over, people on the east end will return wayward goods to the police station to be collected by folks from the west end. Now go make sure your neighbors are getting their kids and their selves inside. I don't want to hear about any fly-aways. We all smell a storm coming, so get going."

As the crowd began their muttering dispersal, Nora Nettle's pickup sputtered into the lot, nearly mowing down newlywed Priscilla Warren, who was not yet used to jumping at the sound of Nora's oncoming truck.

"Durn creaker," cursed Mr. Gamble. "Can't you take her keys, Linden?"

"Already tried, Mac, already tried."

Nora Nettle opened the driver's side door and climbed down.

"Listen to me now," she ordered.

Several people shook their heads and hurried toward home.

"Listen to me *now*!" she screeched, reaching back into her pickup to honk the horn. "Those Klein Boys done took Wilson's Fork and gone over the falls. Most likely they're dead and drowned, but we oughta find 'em anyhow. The mother will want something to bury, don't you know."

"Little Klein didn't go over!" came a voice from the other side of the truck. Emma Brown appeared and hopped into the bed of the truck. "We have him right . . ." she looked under tarps and behind barrels. "He was right here! The dog, too."

Emma Brown's reputation among most adults of Lena was shaky at best, given rumors of her behavior and of her family's misfortunes. Now, finding her in the company of Nora Nettle, standing in an empty pickup, they didn't linger for further explanation.

"Get in," Nora Nettle commanded Emma. She reversed into the quickly parting crowd, chugging back down Main and out of town.

There was only a small gathering left:

Reverend Clambush because he knew that Cornelia would be managing at home just fine and Widow Flom because she didn't have anyone at home. Mac Gamble stayed on because Officer Linden was his cousin, and Muriel the librarian was too frightened of storms to be alone in her apartment above Tim and Tom's Market.

"Mac and Muriel, go get Mrs. Klein and bring her to the police station. Stay downstairs until the storm's over and we find those boys," said Officer Linden.

"Flom and Clambush, let's go." Officer Linden turned on the squad car's light though no one else was out driving, and they sped away.

Farmer Filmore, hurrying to town to check on his widowed sister Dora Flom, had left sheets drying on the line. This got him to thinking about his late wife and how she would not have left sheets on the line in such precarious weather. In fact, she would not have been doing laundry on a Saturday. It was her Monday task.

And on Mondays she always fixed him bacon for breakfast. Farmer Filmore was so lost in Mrs. Filmore thoughts that when he came upon a dog wrapped in a dead bush running toward him, he had to brake fast.

Why, it was the Klein dog. He put his truck in park there in the middle of the road and hopped out.

"Come here, boy! Here, boy!" He crouched down and called LeRoy, who barked and came up to Farmer Filmore whimpering.

"What is it, boy?" Farmer Filmore released LeRoy from the bush, but LeRoy was not satisfied.

He yapped and ran down the road a ways, looking back at Farmer Filmore to follow. He ran into the brush, barked, and looked back.

"Okay, okay, boy! I'm coming." Farmer Filmore left his truck where it was and waded into the brush, into the hush of the forest floor, while up above, the trees groaned under the growing weight of the wind.

Freight Train

When Harold realized he was not to be a dumpling in the river's soup and it was up to him to go for help, his limbs flew into action, rewinding his body across the rock wall — fingers grasping crevices, feet grabbing firm steps. He traced his mind's map as he went: How close was the nearest house? Would someone be home to help him? On this return trip, the wall wasn't as steep as Harold remembered, the ledge not as narrow, the river not as wide. How long would the Bigs be all right in the cave? Two knee bumps, three elbow scrapes, and an unfortunate whap to the nose later, Harold was standing on wet sand and then spread himself out like a contented butterfly on the green grass, on the hard ground, a warm trickle of blood running from nose to ear.

But something was not right. Without moving, Harold looked around him. He listened. There were no birds, no chipmunks, none of the usual forest sounds. Instead there was a hush at the ground. Where were the animals? He rustled some leaves with his foot; he gave a sharp whistle. Nothing stirred. He looked up through the trees to an eerily green sky, then his head filled with a growing roar, like a train, but there were no tracks. What was it Dad always said? If you hear a train and there aren't any tracks, head for the cellar. Tornado.

Little Klein jumped up. He ran from tree to tree. The train was coming closer.

"Mark!" he cried. "Matthew! Luke! LeRoy! Ma! Somebody!"

A big wind was coming and the leaf was alone.

Little Klein looked at that tall wall of water and knew what stood behind. The tornado would come downriver and pass over the falls. There was no time for thinking. Harold Sylvester George Klein stepped back on the ledge. He climbed back behind the falling water and waited.

Harold

Mother Klein paced the basement of the police station. The only places to sit were the beds of the two cells, and she'd offered those to Mac and Muriel. How could they sit at a time like this?

"Do you hear that wind?" she lectured. "The youngest weighs hardly more than the dog." Her whole adult life she'd spent raising these boys and now *poof,* they could be gone in a whoosh of wind. All the work she'd put into protecting her youngest boy, her baby, and then one day she'd just sent him out into the world because she was ornery? It was just like Stanley to be gone at a time like this. Well, she would find her boys.

She started up the steps, but Mr. Gamble stopped her.

"And the falls!" she continued. "They may be impulsive, but my boys would not do something so rash as float a raft above the falls. I told them to stay away from Wilson's Fork and they said they'd stay away from Wilson's Fork and my boys are nothing if not obedient. That Nora Nettle is forever stirring up trouble for my boys." She closed her eyes.

"Lord, get out there and do something to protect my boys. Use that dog if you have to— just don't let them blow away or get smashed by a tree or . . . oh heavens, Lord, just get on now. Please."

Mac Gamble cleared his throat.

"Yes, Mrs. Klein. We all know Nettle. I'm sure she was exaggerating. I'm sure they'll be fine. Now let's just—" but Mr. Gamble's voice was drowned out by Muriel's shriek, which was obliterated by the sound of a freight train passing directly overhead.

Farmer Filmore and LeRoy were nearing the river when they heard the train. As he was a veteran of such storms, Mr. Filmore's heart rate did not change a beat. He simply lifted the dog like a sack of wheat, ran his long-legged run to the bridge, and nestled the two of them on the far side of the cement wall.

Officer Linden and his crew heard the warning, too. They pulled over next to a pickup left in the middle of the road.

"That's Fred's truck!" shouted Widow Flom as they ran for the ditch. "Lordy, lordy. What is Fred doing out in this weather?" The rescue team flattened themselves in the ditch and covered their heads with their arms.

Harold listened to the thundering water. He'd scooted far enough to find the small place where he could sit, draw his knees up to his chin, and grasp a hold of the ledge next to him. The water was now a whisper compared to the greater cry of the wind. The rocks around and under him shuddered, poking like angry fists. Thud after thud, the world trembled. Later, Harold would discover that those thuds were trees coming down in the storm, but at that moment, he felt the earth was breaking apart, leaving him on an island. Water sprayed his face and drenched his clothes. This time he did not cry for help because he knew help could not come. He held fast and waited.

As fast as the train came, it passed, and the world was suddenly still, the water's roar again the largest sound. Harold stood up slowly, touching the back of his bruised head with one hand to make sure he wasn't bleeding. The ledge was slipperier now, and he crept along slowly to the spot where he'd seen his brothers and looked over the edge. There they were, just below him in a cave of sorts, their heads visible at the edge, nearly at the bottom of the falls.

"Guys!" Harold called. "You okay?"

"Little Klein!" Mark called back. "How did you get up there?"

"Walked. Well, climbed a little, slid on my sitter and . . . are you okay?"

"I am, but I don't know about those two. They keep falling asleep like when they conked heads that time. They're breathing, but . . ."

"Can't you get out? " asked Little Klein.

"I'm not sure," said Mark. "It happened so fast. We went over the falls and under at the bottom. We popped up so hard we landed in this cave but barely. I had to drag them in; they were hanging over the edge."

"Is there another way out?"

"I crawled back a ways. There's a sort of tunnel but then more water. We can't slide into the river, and even though we're close to land, I don't see anyplace to step on this side. I guess we'd go your way."

"Stay there," said Harold unnecessarily. "This time I can go get help."

"Be careful!" called Mark.

Again, Harold retraced the now familiar path to sodden ground, whistling his loudest whistle as he went. The forest was not the same forest he'd left not half an hour earlier. Where there had been a small meadow for picnicking, tree carcasses piled atop each other like oversize toothpicks. The top of one old oak lay across the river like a spent dandelion, the remains of the raft caught in her fluff. Harold was an ant moving among these fallen beasts.

He tried whistling for LeRoy, then crawled through the web of roots at the base of some trees, skirted others, and as he scrambled atop the back of a younger oak, his dog came winding through the debris, a soggy cap between his teeth.

"LeRoy!" Harold slid down to the ground, burying his head in LeRoy's damp and smelly neck. "You came back." LeRoy barked and dropped his offering. "Look here," Harold exclaimed. "You found Luke's cap! Good boy!"

"There's one!" cried Widow Flom, and one by one the rescue crew descended on him.

"Put me down," Harold insisted as Widow Flom scooped him up. She squeezed him, then set him down and wiped her eyes.

"You're not too big to be pampered by a relieved old lady," she scolded with a playful pat to his head.

"Come *on*," Harold continued. "My brothers are back there and need help." He led the way along the cluttered riverbank, stopping at the edge of the falls.

"There," he said, pointing with one hand, his other petting LeRoy's insistent snout.

Officer Linden rubbed his bald head, his beloved police hat long gone with the wind.

Harold stepped closer to the falling water.

"Don't!" cried Reverend Clambush and Widow Flom, grabbing for him at once.

But they were not quick enough. Just as Nora Nettle arrived, leading Mother Klein, Muriel, Mac Gamble, and Mean Emma Brown, he disappeared from view, LeRoy yapping wildly at the water.

"Where are my boys?" demanded Mother Klein. "Why are you all standing around? What's being done?"

Harold stepped out on the grass next to the falls and LeRoy. There was a collective gasp.

"Come on!" he shouted. "There's a cave in the wall behind the falls. My brothers are in it."

The adults stood with mouths gaping, but Emma Brown didn't hesitate. She scrambled up next to Little Klein, and soon she disappeared as well.

Mother Klein grabbed Widow Flom's hand and the two of them followed Emma's steps. They planted themselves next to LeRoy, peering into the water.

"I'm going in," said Mother Klein. She pulled at her shoes without unlacing them.

"Oh, no you don't, Esther." Widow Flom took Mother Klein's arm, then held her close. "Sing yourself a sturdy song, but you'll help 'em more by staying on dry land. Here, I'll start. *Shall we gather at the river . . .*"

LeRoy howled.

Behind the falls, Harold navigated with Emma right behind him. He studied the distance between their ledge and the cave.

"Mark, can you stand up?" Harold called.

"I think so," he answered. The mouth of the cave jutted far enough out that his head cleared the rocks above him. "It's wet, though, and slippery. If you're coming down, you should take off your shoes."

Emma slid down to sit beside him on the ledge and said, "I'll get your shoes."

Harold yelped and sidestepped away.

"Give me your foot, runt. I'm trying to help you," Emma growled. Harold considered his options. He was behind a wall of rushing water with Mean Emma Brown on one side and a slick shelf of rock on the other. He stepped back and closed his eyes. Emma unlaced his shoes and held them down while Harold lifted out his feet.

"Now what are you waiting for?" she demanded.

Harold glanced down at Emma Brown. She hadn't yanked his shoes out from under him. She hadn't pushed him over the edge. Actually sitting there next to him, holding his shoes, puzzling over their dilemma, Emma Brown looked a lot like a regular girl. Harold tried to remember what it was that made her so mean, but aside from his brothers saying so, he couldn't come up with anything. Still, a fellow had to be careful.

"I'm fine," he squeaked. "You can go back."

Without a word, Emma stood and edged back to land, carrying his shoes.

"Okay," he called to Mark. "What now?"

"Ask for the doctor. But first, come down here," Mark answered, "and we'll figure out how to get Matthew and Luke out." Mark pointed out bumps and ledges for stepping and holding.

"That will work," Harold said, crouching in the cave. "I'll go get help." He scuttled up and out, where he met the waiting rescuers.

"We need Dr. Dahlke," he said, then added

hastily, "Nothing bad, Mother. They're okay. Really. Matthew and Luke bumped their heads. We figured out how to get them all out."

"Are they screaming in pain?" asked Widow Flom.

"No," said Harold.

"Are any of their limbs hanging off in unnatural directions?"

"Uh . . ."

"They're moving around, right?"

Harold nodded. "A little."

"We don't need Dr. Dahlke. They've probably got themselves a heap of bruises and a couple of mild concussions.

"Are you okay in there, Mark?" she bellowed, but if he heard her, his response was lost in the falling water. "Harold, you and Mark keep those other two awake. Soon as they can get up without being dizzy or throwing up, you start showing them the way out."

And so they waited. Mother Klein, LeRoy, and Emma on the grass; Mark and Harold back in the cave, shaking Matthew and Luke whenever their eyelids fell. They splashed muddy water on them to hurry the process along, then started slowly out of the cave, Harold leading the way. He showed his brothers which rocks to step on, which knobs to grab for support. One by one the boys emerged on the grass and everyone rushed to them.

Harold slipped out of the sea of arms that was hugging and holding up his brothers. Mother Klein turned and caught his elbow, spinning him back to the group.

"Here's the biggest of the Kleins today," she said.

LeRoy sniffed through the assembly. His boys were all there. He brushed between and around Matthew's legs, then circled Luke around and around with a triplet of barks. He jumped up on Mark's chest and licked the face Mark bent to him. LeRoy bounded up to Little Klein and back to the Bigs.

"Shiner!" exclaimed Luke, putting his hand up to his bruised face.

"My baby," crooned Mother Klein as the

whole party started their parade through downed branches and trees to the road.

Harold and Emma lagged behind. As they passed the bridge, approaching a fallen tree whose branches nested a jumble of broken boards, Harold drew up his last sip of courage. "Can you help me with something?" he said to two large brown boots.

"What do you want, Little Klein?" Emma Brown boomed.

"Harold," he objected, and, when met with no bodily harm, looked up at Emma Brown's face, its hard surface softening nearly into a smile.

"What do you want, Harold?"

"There's a raft in that tree. Will you help me get it down?"

"What are you going to do with a broken-down raft, Harold Klein?" she asked.

"I'm going to use the boards to build a tree house."